MISTY OF CHINCOTEAGUE

MISTY
OF CHINCOTEAGUE

By MARGUERITE HENRY

Illustrated by Wesley Dennis

Aladdin Paperbacks

Aladdin Paperbacks
An imprint of Simon & Schuster
Children's Publishing Division
1230 Avenue of the Americas
New York, NY 10020
Copyright © 1947, copyright © renewed 1975 by Marguerite Henry.
Illustrations copyright © 1947, copyright © renewed 1975
by Morgan and Charles Reid Dennis
All rights reserved including the right of reproduction
in whole or in part in any form.
First Aladdin Paperbacks edition 1991
10 9 8 7 6 5 4 3 2 1

Printed in the United States of America

Library of Congress Cataloging-in-Publication Data
Henry, Marguerite, 1902-
    Misty of Chincoteague / by Marguerite Henry; illustrated by
Wesley Dennis. — 1st Aladdin Books ed.
        p.   cm.
    Summary: The determination of two youngsters to win a Chincoteague
pony is greatly increased when the Phantom and her colt are among
those rounded up for the yearly auction.
    ISBN 0-689-84512-X
    1. Chincoteague pony—Juvenile fiction.   [1. Chincoteague pony—
Fiction.   2. Ponies—Fiction.   3. Chincoteague Island (Va.)—
Fiction.]   I. Dennis, Wesley, ill.   II. Title.
PZ10.3.H43Mg   1991   [Fic]—dc20   90-27237   CIP   AC

To
Paul and Maureen Beebe
Grandpa and Grandma Beebe
Eba Jones, Fire Chief
Wyle Maddox, Leader of Roundup Men
L. Quillen, Roundup Man
Wilbur Wimbrow, Roundup Man
Howard Rodgers, Roundup Man
Harvey Beebe, Roundup Man
Harold Beebe, father of Paul and Maureen
Ralph Beebe, uncle of Paul and Maureen
Delbert Daisey, Bronc Buster
Victoria and William Pruitt

all of whom really live on Chincoteague Island
and who appear as characters in this book

and a special dedication to
Three Chincoteague Ponies
Phantom
Pied Piper
Misty

All the incidents in this story are real. They did not happen in just the order they are recorded, but they all happened at one time or another on the little island of Chincoteague.

CONTENTS

PART ONE

BEFORE MISTY

Chapter 1

LIVE CARGO!

A WILD, ringing neigh shrilled up from the hold of the Spanish galleon. It was not the cry of an animal in hunger. It was a terrifying bugle. An alarm call.

The captain of the *Santo Cristo* strode the poop deck. "Cursed be that stallion!" he muttered under his breath as he stamped forward and back, forward and back.

Suddenly he stopped short. The wind! It was dying with the sun. It was spilling out of the sails, causing them to quiver and shake. He could feel his flesh creep with the sails. Without wind he could not get to Panama. And if he did not get there, and get there soon, he was headed for trouble. The Moor ponies to be delivered to the Viceroy of Peru could not be kept alive much longer. Their hay had grown musty. The water casks were almost empty. And now this sudden calm, this heavy warning of a storm.

He plucked nervously at his rusty black beard as if that would help him think. "We lie in the latitude of white squalls," he said, a look of vexation on his face. "When the wind does strike, it will strike with fury." His steps quickened. "We must shorten sail," he made up his mind.

Cupping his hands to his mouth, he bellowed orders: "Furl the topgallant sail! Furl the coursers and the main-topsail! Shorten the fore-topsail!"

The ship burst into action. From forward and aft all hands came running. They fell to work furiously, carrying out orders.

The captain's eyes were fixed on his men, but his thoughts raced ahead to the rich land where he was bound. In his mind's eye he could see the mule train coming to meet him when he reached land. He could see it snaking its way along the Gold Road from Panama to the seaport of Puerto Bello. He could almost feel the smooth, hard gold in the packs on the donkeys' backs.

His eyes narrowed greedily. "Gold!" he mumbled. "Think of trading twenty ponies for their weight in gold!" He clasped his hands behind him and resumed his pacing and muttering. "The Viceroy of Peru sets great store by the ponies, and well he may. Without the ponies to work the mines, there will be no more gold." Then he clenched his fists. "We must keep the ponies alive!"

His thoughts were brought up sharply. That shrill horse call! Again it filled the air about him with a wild ring. His beady eyes darted to the lookout man in the crow's-nest, then to the men on deck. He saw fear spread among the crew.

Meanwhile, in the dark hold of the ship, a small bay stallion was pawing the floor of his stall. His iron shoes with their sharp rims and turned-down heels threw a shower of sparks, and he felt strong charges of electricity. His nostrils flared. The moisture in the air! The charges of electricity! These were storm warnings—things he knew. Some inner urge told him he must get his mares to high land before the storm broke. He tried to escape, charging against the chest board of his stall again and again. He threw his head back and bugled.

From stalls beside him and from stalls opposite him, nineteen heads with small pointed ears peered out. Nineteen pairs of brown eyes whited. Nineteen young mares caught his anxiety. They, too, tried to escape, rearing and plunging, rearing and plunging.

But presently the animals were no longer hurling themselves. They were *being* hurled. The ship was pitching and tossing to the rising swell of the sea, flinging the ponies forward against their chest boards, backward against the ship's sides.

A cold wind spiraled down the hatch. It whistled and screamed above the rough voice of the captain. It gave way only to the deep *flump-flump* of the thunder.

The sea became a wildcat now, and the galleon her prey. She stalked the ship and drove her off her course. She slapped at her, rolling her victim from side to side. She knocked the spars out of her and used them to ram holes in her sides. She

14

clawed the rudder from its sternpost and threw it into the sea. She cracked the ship's ribs as if they were brittle bones. Then she hissed and spat through the seams.

The pressure of the sea swept everything before it. Huge baskets filled with gravel for ballast plummeted down the passageway between the ponies, breaking up stalls as they went by.

Suddenly the galleon shuddered. From bow to stern came an endless rasping sound! The ship had struck a shoal. And with a ripping and crashing of timber the hull cracked open. In that split second the captain, his men, and his live cargo were washed into the boiling foam.

The wildcat sea yawned. She swallowed the men. Only the captain and fifteen ponies managed to come up again. The captain bobbed alongside the stallion and made a wild grasp for his tail, but a great wave swept him out of reach.

The stallion neighed encouragement to his mares, who were struggling to keep afloat, fighting the wreckage and the sea. For long minutes they thrashed about helplessly, and just when their strength was nearly spent, the storm died as suddenly as it had risen. The wind calmed.

The sea was no longer a wildcat. She became a kitten, fawning and lapping about the ponies' legs. Now their hooves touched land. They were able to stand! They were scrambling up the beach, up on Assateague Beach, that long, sandy island which shelters the tidewater country of Virginia and Maryland. They were far from the mines of Peru.

Chapter 2

THE ISLAND OF THE WILD THINGS

THE PONIES were exhausted and their coats were heavy with water, but they were free, free, *free!* They raised their heads and snuffed the wind. The smell was unlike that of the lowland moors of Spain, but it was good! They sucked in the sharp, sweet pungence of pine woods, and somewhere mixed in with the piney smell came the enticing scent of salt grass.

Their stomachs were pinched with hunger, but the ponies did not seek the grass at once. They shook the water from their coats. Then they rolled back and forth in the sand, enjoying the solid feel of the land.

17

At last the stallion's hunger stirred him to action. He rounded up his mares, and with only a watery moon to light the way, he drove them through the needle-carpeted woods. The mares stopped to eat the leaves of some myrtle bushes, but the stallion jostled them into line. Then he took the lead. So direct was his progress it seemed almost as if he had trodden here before. Through bramble and thicket, through brackish pools of water, he led the way.

The moon was high overhead when the little band came out on grassy marshland. They stopped a moment to listen to the wide blades of grass whisper and squeak in the wind; to sniff the tickling smell of salt grass.

This was it! This was the exciting smell that had urged them on. With wild snorts of happiness they buried their noses in the long grass. They bit and tore great mouthfuls—frantically, as if they were afraid it might not last. Oh, the salty goodness of it! Not bitter at all, but juicy-sweet with rain. It was different from any grass they knew. It billowed and shimmered like the sea. They could not get enough of it. That delicious salty taste! Never had they known anything like it. Never. And sometimes they came upon tender patches of lespedeza, a kind of clover that grew among the grasses.

The ponies forgot the forty days and forty nights in the dark hold of the Spanish galleon. They forgot the musty hay. They forgot the smell of bilge water, of oil and fishy odors from the cooking galley.

When they could eat no more, they pawed shallow wells with their hooves for drinking water. Then they rolled in the wiry grass, letting out great whinnies of happiness. They seemed unable to believe that the island was all their own. Not a human being anywhere. Only grass. And sea. And sky. And the wind.

At last they slept.

The seasons came and went, and the ponies adopted the New World as their own. They learned how to take care of themselves. When summer came and with it the greenhead flies by day and the mosquitoes by night, they plunged into the sea, up to their necks in the cool surf. The sea was their *friend*. Once it had set them free. Now it protected them from their fiercest enemies.

Winter came and the grass yellowed and dried, but the ponies discovered that close to the roots it was still green and good to eat.

Even when a solid film of ice sealed the land, they did not go hungry. They broke through the ice with their hooves or went off to the woods to eat the myrtle leaves that stayed green all winter.

Snow was a new experience, too. They blew at it, making little snow flurries of their own. They tasted it. It melted on their tongues. Snow was good to drink!

If the Spaniards could have seen their ponies now, they would have been startled at their changed appearance. No longer were their coats sleek. They were as thick and shaggy as the coat of any sheep dog. This was a good thing. On bitter days, when they stood close-huddled for comfort, each pony could enjoy the added warmth of his neighbor's coat as well as his own.

There were no wolves or wildcats on the island, but there was deep, miry mud to trap creatures and suck them down. After a few desperate struggles, the ponies learned how to fall to their knees, then sidle and wriggle along like crabs until they were well out of it.

With each season the ponies grew wiser. And with each season they became tougher and more hardy. Horse colts and fillies were born to them. As the horse colts grew big, they rounded up mares of their own and started new herds that ranged wild—wild as the wind and the sea that had brought them there long ago.

Years went by. And more years. Changes came to Assateague. The red men came. The white men came. The white men built a lighthouse to warn ships of dangerous reefs. They built a handful of houses and a white church. But soon the houses stood empty. The people moved their homes and their church to nearby Chincoteague Island, for Assateague belonged to the wild things—to the wild birds that nested on it, and the wild ponies whose ancestors had lived on it since the days of the Spanish galleon.

PART TWO

MISTY OF CHINCOTEAGUE

Chapter 3

THE PHANTOM

SPRING TIDES had come once more to Assateague Island. They were washing and salting the earth, coaxing new green spears to replace the old dried grasses.

On a windy Saturday morning, half-past March, a boy and his sister were toiling up the White Hills of Assateague Beach. The boy was taller than the girl and led the way. Their progress was slow. The heavy beach sand seemed to pull them back, as if it felt that human beings had no right to be there.

In the early morning light the two figures were scarcely visible. Their faded play clothes were the color of sand and their hair was bleached pale by the sun. The boy's hair had a way of falling down over his brow like the forelock of a stallion. The girl's streamed out behind her, a creamy golden mane with the wind blowing through it.

Suddenly the boy bent over and picked up a whitened, bow-shaped object. The girl was at his side in an instant.

"What is it, Paul?"

The boy did not answer. He kept feeling the object, running his fingers over it, testing the weight of it. Then he squinted

his eyes against the sun and looked out upon the thin line of blue where the sky and the sea met.

"Is it the bone of a horse?"

Paul looked down his nose in disgust. "Maureen," he shook his head, "aren't you ever going to grow up?"

"Is it an Indian bow washed white by the sea?" the girl persisted.

Paul hardly heard. His eyes were scanning the horizon.

"See a ship?" Maureen asked.

"Hmm," he nodded.

"I don't see anything. Where, Paul? What kind of ship?"

"A Spanish galleon," he said. "She's caught in a northeaster. Look at her pitch!"

"Oh, Paul," fretted the girl. "You are always play-acting." Then she added wistfully, "I hanker to see the things you see. Tell me what the ship's like. Make it a whopper."

"Can't see her now. She's lost in the swell."

He pushed the hair out of his eyes. "There she is!" he gasped, enjoying his own make-believe. "Her sails painted gold and there's a gold horse with wings at her prow. She's heading toward the shoals. She's going to crack up!"

"Oh, Paul!"

"What's more, she's carrying live cargo! Horses! And they're feared of the storm. I can hear 'em crying and screeching above the wind." He turned abruptly to his sister. "Now can you guess what I just found?"

"No. What?"

"Why, a rib bone, you goose. A rib bone of the Spanish galleon that was wrecked." Paul braced his legs in the sand and watched his sister's face. The result pleased him. Her eyes and mouth flew open.

"This is part of her hull. Fact is, it's her bones that caused the sands to drift higher and higher 'til they formed the White Hills we're standing on."

The girl looked around and about her. Everything was still and quiet on little Assateague Island. Their grandfather had brought the game warden to the island in his boat, and she and Paul had asked to come along. But now she wondered if they should have come. The men were seeing how the wild birds had weathered the winter. They were far to the north. No other creatures were in sight. Suddenly she felt a little chill of fear.

"Paul," she asked in a hushed voice, "do you feel like we're trespassing?"

Paul nodded. "If you look close," he whispered, "you can see that the wild critters have 'No Trespassing' signs tacked up on every pine tree."

"I wasn't thinking about the wild things," Maureen replied. She shielded her eyes against the sun and looked off in the direction of Tom's Cove. "Wish Grandpa'd come to take us back home to Chincoteague. It seems spooky-like to be exploring a ship's graveyard."

"I like exploring. I don't care if . . ."

Suddenly, from the pine thicket behind them came the sharp crackling of underbrush. Paul wheeled around, his eyes darting to an open glade.

"Watch the open place, Maureen! It's the Pied Piper and his band!"

With manes and tails flying, a band of wild ponies swept into the natural grazing ground. A pinto stallion was in command. He bunched his mares, then tossed his head high, searching the wind.

29

Paul and Maureen fell to the sand. They did not want the wind to carry their scent. They watched as the stallion herded his family like a nervous parent on a picnic. When he made certain that no one was missing, he began browsing. It was like a signal. His mares lowered their heads and settled down to the business of grazing.

Paul's eyes were fixed on the wild horses. They were cropping grass peacefully. But he knew that one strange sound would send them rocketing off into the woods. He and Maureen spoke softly, and scarcely moved.

"Do y'see the Phantom?" asked Maureen.

The very mention of the name "Phantom" set Paul's heart thumping against the walls of his chest. That mysterious wild mare about whom so many stories were told!

"No," he answered. "They're bunched too close."

"Do you reckon the Phantom's real? Or do you reckon it was some sea monster upset that boat last roundup?"

Paul gave no answer. Was the Phantom real? Sometimes he wondered. She had never been captured, and the roundup men did sometimes tell tall tales. Some had said she was a dark creature, dark and mysterious, like the pine trees. And some said she was the color of copper, with splashes of silver in her mane and tail. And some spoke of a strange white marking that began at her withers and spread out like a white map of the United States.

"Maybe," whispered Maureen, "maybe she got poor and died off during the winter."

"Her?" scoffed Paul, his eyes never leaving the herd. "Not her! Any pony that can outsmart Grandpa and all the roundup men for two years running can rustle her feed, all right. Recommember how Uncle Jed said his horse broke a leg trying to follow the Phantom at the roundup last Pony Penning Day?"

"Wish girls could go along on the roundup; maybe she wouldn't bolt away from another girl."

Paul snorted. "She'd leap into the waves and swim out to sea just like she did last year and the year before that." Then suddenly his face lighted as if an idea had just struck him. "But this year it's going to be different."

"Why is it?"

"Because," Paul replied, gripping the rib bone in his hand, "because I'm old enough to go with the roundup men this year. That's why. And if there *is* such a filly, I'm going to get her, and on Pony Penning Day she'll be in the corral with the others."

"For sale?"

"No, I'll tie a rope around her neck to show she's already sold. To me. To us," he added hastily, thinking of the cost of her. "She'll sell for around a hundred dollars, maybe."

"Oh, Paul! Let me help."

"All right, I will. How much money can you earn between now and Pony Penning Day?"

Maureen drew a quick breath. "I can earn as much as any boy. I can rake clams and gather oysters, and I can catch soft-shell crabs, and if Grandma doesn't need me, I suppose I could clean out people's chicken houses. I won't mind the work if ever we could *keep* a pony for our very own."

A little silence fell between them as they lay on their stomachs in the sand, their eyes fastened on the herd.

"I reckon we'd better keep our plans to ourselves," Paul spoke at last. "Then, if we don't get her—"

"Then nobody can poke fingers at us and laugh," finished Maureen. "Paul . . ."

"Hmm?"

"Why does everyone in school think we're lucky to live on Grandpa's pony ranch? Why is it?"

Paul was busy with thoughts of the Phantom.

"Do you reckon," Maureen went on, remembering to keep her voice low, "do you reckon it's because their families are watermen instead of horsemen?"

"Maybe."

"Or is it because Papa and Mama are in China and they think grandparents aren't as strict as parents?"

Paul was in a dream. He was capturing the mysterious wild mare. He was listening to Maureen with only half his mind.

"I reckon it's the ponies," he said at last. "But what fun is it to gentle a wild colt and just when he learns that you're his friend, Grandpa sells him and you never see him again?"

"I can't abide it either," said Maureen; "but there's something hurts worse."

"What?"

"It's when the colts are sold, right out from under their mothers. I get sick inside watching it."

"That's because you're a girl."

Suddenly Paul leaped to his feet. "Look!" he cried as a red streak broke from the herd and went crashing into the woods. "It's the Phantom! I saw the white map on her withers. I did. I did!"

For a full minute the pony was lost among the pines. Then out she came heading toward the White Hills. Behind her whipped the Pied Piper, and his ringing cry was a command.

"Run, Maureen! Run! He's a killer."

The boy and his sister flew down the hill, stumbling over dried brush and blackberry vines. As they reached the beach, they turned back and watched, breathless. Pied Piper was overtaking the Phantom. He was running alongside her. Now he was twisting into the air, lacing her with his forefeet. They could hear the dull pounding of his hooves against her body. Then they saw the Phantom turn. They saw the droop of her tail as she gave up her dash for freedom and meekly followed the stallion into the woods.

Long seconds after they were gone, the air seemed to quiver with the Pied Piper's bugle.

"I hate him!" cried Maureen, bursting into tears. "I hate him! I hate him!"

"Quit acting like a girl, Maureen! Pied Piper knows she's better off with the band. Even the Phantom knows it. Grandpa says horses got to stick together for protection. Same as people."

Chapter 4

SACRED BONES

H ALL-OO-OO!" came a voice down the beach. The boy and the girl turned to see Grandpa Beebe swinging toward them, his gnarled arms upraised like a wind-twisted tree.

"Paul!" he boomed. "Put down that bone. Put it down, I tell ye!"

Paul had forgotten all about the curved piece of wood. Now he noticed that he was clenching it so tightly it left a white streak in the palm of his hand. He dropped it quickly as Grandpa came up.

"How often do I got to tell you that bones is sacred? Even ship's bones."

"Is it true, Grandpa?" asked Paul.

"Be what true?" Grandpa repeated, pulling off his battered felt hat and letting the wind toss his hair.

"About the Spanish galleon being wrecked . . ."

"And the ponies swimming ashore?" added Maureen.

Grandpa Beebe squinted at the sun. "It's nigh onto noontide," he said, "and your Grandma is having sixteen head to dinner tomorrow. We got to get back home to Chincoteague right smart quick! I promised to kill some turkeys for her." He sighed heavily. "Seems as if the devil is allus sittin' cross-legged of me."

But he made no move to go. Instead, he squatted down on the beach, muttering, "Don't see why she's got to parboil 'em today." Then he took off his boots and socks and dug his toes in the sand, like fiddler crabs scuttling for home.

"Feels good, don't it?" he said, with a grin. He looked from Paul to Maureen and back again. "Yer know," he went on, and he began to rub the bristles of his ear, as he always did when he was happy. "Yer know, the best thing about havin' fourteen head of children is ye're bound to get one or two good grandchildren outen the lot."

"Grandpa!" reminded Paul. "Is it true about the Spanish galleon and the ponies? Or is it a legend like the folks over on the mainland say?"

38

"'Course it's true!" replied Grandpa, with a little show of irritation. "All the wild herds on Assateague be descendants of a bunch of Spanish hosses. They wasn't wild to begin with, mind ye. They just went wild with their freedom."

Maureen did a quick little leap, like a colt bucking.

"Then it's *not* a legend?" she rejoiced. "It's *not* a legend!"

"Who said 'twasn't a legend?" Grandpa exclaimed. "'Course it's a legend. But legends be the only stories as is true!"

He stopped to find the right words. "Facts are fine, fer as they go," he said, "but they're like water bugs skittering atop the water. Legends, now—they go deep down and bring up the heart of a story." Here Grandpa shoved his hand into the pocket of his overalls and produced a long stick of licorice and a plug of tobacco. With a pair of wire clippers he divided the licorice in half and gave a piece to Maureen and one to Paul. Then he cut himself a quid of tobacco.

There was a little silence while the old man and the boy and the girl thought about the shipwrecked ponies.

Then, almost in the same breath, Paul and Maureen blurted out together: "Who discovered 'em?"

Grandpa spat out to sea. "Why, I heard tell 'twas the Indians chanced on 'em first. They comes over to hunt on Assateague, and 'twasn't only deer and otter and beaver they finds. They finds these wild ponies pawin' the air and snortin' through their noses, and they ain't never seed no critters like that, blowin' steam and screamin' and their tails and manes a-flyin'. And the Indians was so affrighted they run for their canoes."

Grandpa Beebe began rubbing both ears in his excitement.

"Then what, Grandpa?"

"Why, the ponies was left to run wilder and wilder. Nobody lived here to hinder 'em none, nobody at all. White men come to live on our Chincoteague Island, but Assateague was left to the critters."

40

Grandpa reached for one of his socks, then broke out in sudden laughter. "Ho! Ho! Ho!" he bellowed.

Paul and Maureen looked all around them. "What's so funny, Grandpa?" they asked.

Grandpa was slapping his thigh, rocking back and forth. "I jes' now thought of somethin' right smart cute," he chuckled, when he could get his breath. "Y'see, lots of folks like to call theirselves descendants of the First Families of Virginia. They kinda makes a high-falutin' club outen it and labels it F.F.V. But you know what?" Here Grandpa's eyes twinkled like the sea with the sun blazing on it.

"What?" chorused Paul and Maureen.

"The real first families of Virginia was the ponies! Ho-ho-ho! That's what *my* history book says!"

"Whee! Grandpa!" exclaimed Paul. "I like the way you talk about history."

Grandpa winked in agreement. "Nothin' so exciting as tag ends pulled right outen the core of the past."

"Did the first white men tame the ponies?" asked Maureen.

"No indeedy. Them first white men had no use fer the wild, thrashin' ponies. A slow-going pair o' oxen could do all the plowin' for bread corn and sech. Guess mebbe it was Bob Watson's boy of Chincoteague who fust tried to put a wild pony to plow. She was a dead ringer for the Phantom, too. But that was a long time agone."

Paul's heart turned a somersault.

"What happened to her, Grandpa? Did she gentle?"

"Did she gentle! Why, she jes' broke the singletree as if 'twas a matchstick, cleared the fence, and blew to her island home with the reins a-stringin' out behind her."

"Oh!"

"Some of 'em you jest can't gentle. Not after they've lived wild. Only the youngsters is worth botherin' about, so far as the gentlin' goes. Recommember that!"

Paul and Maureen looked at each other. They were thinking of their secret plan to own the Phantom.

Grandpa Beebe began putting on his socks and shoes. "Likely the game warden is done checkin' up on the wild birds. I promised to meet him at Tom's Cove afore the tide ebbs bare. But," he added, as he pulled on his boots, "I know my tides, and I'll give ye time for one more question."

Maureen looked to Paul. "You ask, Paul."

Paul jumped to his feet. How could he ask just one question when dozens popped into his mind? He began picking up fiddler crabs furiously, as if that would help him think. Finally he turned to Grandpa.

"It's about Pony Penning Day," he blurted out. "How did it start?"

It was plain to see that Grandpa Beebe liked the question. He began rubbing the bristles of one ear and then the other. "'Twas this-a-way," he said. "In the yesterdays, when their corn was laid by, folks on Chincoteague got to yearnin' fer a big hollerday. So they sails over to Assateague and rounds up all the wild ponies. 'Twas big sport."

"Like hunting buffalo or deer?" asked Paul.

"'Zactly like that! Only they didn't kill the ponies; just rounded 'em up for the fun of the chase. Then they cut out a few of the younglings to gentle, tried some ropin' and rough ridin' of the wild ones, et a big dinner of out-door pot pie, and comes on back home to Chincoteague. By-'n-by, they adds somethin' to the fun. They swum the ponies acrost the channel to Chincoteague and put on a big show. 'Twas so excitin', folks come from as far as New York to see it. And afore we knowed it, we was sellin' off some of the colts to the mainlanders."

"Why did they sell the wild things?" asked Maureen.

"Why!" echoed Grandpa. "Why, ponies was overrunnin' Assateague. They was gettin' thick as raisins in a pie!"

"That thick, Grandpa?" asked Maureen, her eyes rounded.

"Wal, maybe not that thick," grinned Grandpa.

"Don't keep interrupting Grandpa!" exclaimed Paul.

"Today it's jest the same," Grandpa said slowly. "Along toward the tail end of July, when the ponies is done with fightin' and foalin' and the watermen is tired of plantin' oysters, then we all get to hankerin' for a celebration. So the menfolk round up the ponies, the womenfolk bake meat pot pie, and there ye are! Only now, outside a few hossmen like me, the fire department owns most of the wild ponies. And a good thing it is for Chincoteague."

"Why is it?"

"'Cause all the money they make from sellin' 'em goes into our fire-fightin' apparatus."

44

Grandpa Beebe rose stiffly. "Come on, you two, I hain't got time to school ye. That's what me and Grandma pays taxes for. Besides, we been a-settin' here so long the sand is liable to drift up over us and make another white clift outen us. It's time we was gettin' back home to Chincoteague, and Grandma's turkeys."

Chapter 5

A PIECE OF WIND AND SKY

APRIL, May, June, July! Only four months until Pony Penning Day. Only four months to plan and work for the Phantom.

Suddenly Time was important.

"We got to lay a course and hold it," said Paul, as he whisked over the fence that same afternoon and began studying the ponies in Grandpa Beebe's corral.

Maureen slipped between the rails and caught up with him. "Quit talking like a waterman, Paul. Talk like a horseman so I can understand you."

"All right, I will. Grandpa's got eleven mares here. Six of 'em have a colt apiece, and the black and the chestnut each have a yearling and a suckling. Between now and July, how many colts do you reckon Grandpa will sell?"

"Probably all of 'em—except the sucklings, of course."

"That's what I figure! Now if we could halter-break the colts and teach 'em some manners, folks'd pay more for them, wouldn't they?"

"I reckon."

"All right!" exclaimed Paul as he sailed back over the fence. "Maybe Grandpa will pay us the difference."

That night at the supper table Paul looked up over his plate of roast oysters and caught Grandma's eye.

"Grandma," he questioned, "do you like a mannerly colt?"

Grandma Beebe's face was round as a holly berry and soft little whiskers grew about her mouth, like the feelers of a very young colt. She pursed her lips now, wondering if there were some catch to Paul's question.

"Paul means," explained Maureen, "if you came here to Pony Ranch to buy a colt, would you choose one that was gentled or would you choose a wild one?"

Grandpa clucked. "Can't you jes' see yer Grandma crowhoppin' along on a wild colt!"

"Thar's yer answer," laughed Grandma, as she cut golden squares of cornbread. "I'd take the mannerly colt."

Paul swallowed a plump oyster, almost choking in his haste. "Would you," he gulped, "that is, would you be willing to pay out more money for it, Grandma?"

"Wa-al, that depends," mused Grandma, passing the breadboard around, "that depends on how *much* more."

"Would you pay ten dollars more?"

"If he was nice and mannerly, I would. Yes, I would."

"See there, Grandpa!" The words came out in a rush. "If Maureen and I was to halter-break the colts, could we—" He stopped, and then stammered, "Could we have the ten extra dollars for each colt sold?"

So dead a silence fell over the table that the *drip-drip* of the kitchen faucet sounded like hammer strokes.

Grandpa slowly buttered his bread and then glanced about the table.

"Pass your Grandpa the goody, Maureen."

All eyes watched Grandpa spread a layer of wild black-berry jam on top of the butter. Then he added another square of cornbread to make a sandwich. Not until he had tasted and approved did he turn to Paul.

"What fer?" he barked.

Paul and Maureen stared at their plates.

"Must be a secret, Clarence," Grandma pleaded.

Grandpa swept a few crumbs into his hand and began stacking his own dishes. "I ain't never pried a secret outa no one," he said. "And I don't aim to start pokin' and pryin' now. It's a deal, children, and ye don't need to tell me whut the money's fer until ye're ready to spend it."

Paul and Maureen flew to Grandpa and hugged him. For a moment they forgot that they were almost grown up.

The days and weeks that followed were not half long enough. Up at dawn, working with the colts, haltering them, teaching them to lead and to stand tied! Going to school regretfully and hurrying home as soon as it was out!

Now when a buyer came to look at the colts, Maureen did not run to her room as she used to do, pressing her face in the feather bed to stifle her sobs. Nor did Paul swing up on one of Grandpa's ponies and gallop down the hard point of land to keep from crying. Now they actually led the colts out to the buyers to show how gentle they were. They even helped load them onto waiting trucks. All the while they kept thinking that soon they would have a pony of their own, never to be sold. *Not for any price.*

April and May passed. School closed.

Paul and Maureen worked furiously for the Phantom. They caught and sold crabs. They gathered oysters when the tide went out and laid the oyster rocks bare. And most exciting of all, they "treaded for clams." In flannel moccasins to protect their feet, and wide-brimmed hats on their heads, they plunged into Chincoteague Bay. Sometimes they would whinny and snort, pretending they were wild ponies escaping the flies. Then suddenly they would feel the thin edge of a clam with their feet and remember that they were clam treaders, trying to earn money for the Phantom.

Paul learned how to burrow under the sand with his toes and lift the clam to the surface on the top of his moccasined

foot. But try as she would, Maureen never could do it. She raked the clams instead, with a long wooden rake. Then she dumped them into a home-made basket formed by spreading a piece of canvas inside an old inner tube. She kept it from floating out to sea by tying it to her waist with a rope.

Slowly, week by week, Grandpa's old tobacco pouch in which they stored their money began to round out, until it held exactly one hundred dollars. It never occurred to Paul and Maureen that the Phantom might escape the roundup men this year, too. They felt as certain of owning her as if someone had sent them a telegram that read,

SHIPPING YOUR PONY ON PONY PENNING DAY=

One early morning, when July was coming in, Paul cornered Grandpa hustling across the barnyard. He stepped right into Grandpa's path so that he had to stop short.

"Grandpa!" Paul burst out. "Will you rent me one of your empty stalls beginning with Pony Penning Day? I'll do a man's work to pay for it."

Grandpa roughed his hand up the back of Paul's head. 'Who you want it fer, lad? Plan to sleep in it yourself?"

Paul's face turned red. "I," he hesitated. "That is, Maureen and I are going to . . ."

"Wa-al?"

"We're going to buy—we're going to buy the Phantom on Pony Penning Day."

There! The news was out!

Grandpa threw back his head. He opened wide his mouth, ready to break out in laughter, but when he saw the grave look in Paul's eyes, he did not laugh at all. Instead, he let out a shrill "Wee-dee-dee-dee, wee-dee-dee-dee," as he pulled a handful of corn out of his pocket and spattered the golden kernels about his feet.

From all over the barnyard came wild geese and tame geese, big ducks and little ducks, marsh hens and chicks. The air was wild with the clatter they made.

"Can't no one catch the Phantom," Grandpa yelled above the noise. "For two years she's give the horse laugh to the best roundup men we got on Chincoteague. What makes ye think she's going to *ask* to be caught?"

"Because," Paul shouted through the din, "because the Fire Chief promised I could go along this year."

Grandpa Beebe stepped back a pace and studied his grandson. His clear eyes twinkled with merriment. Then a look of pity crossed his face.

"Lad," he said, "the Phantom don't wear that white map on her withers for nothing. It stands for Liberty, and ain't no human being going to take her liberty away from her."

"She wants to come to us," Paul said, trying to keep his voice steady. "Ever since that day on Assateague, Maureen and I knew."

A white striker bird flew up from the ground and perched on Grandpa's gnarled forefinger. Grandpa directed his remarks to the bird. "Can't fer the life of me see why those two want another pony Why, the corral's full of 'em. They're as much Paul's and Maureen's as anybody's."

Paul's lips tightened. "It's not the same," he said. "Owning a pony you never have to sell . . ."

The striker bird flew away. Paul and Grandpa watched in silence as it dipped and rose to the sky.

Grandpa stood in thought. "Paul boy," he said slowly, "hark to my words. The Phantom ain't a hoss. She ain't even a lady. She's just a piece of wind and sky."

Paul tried to speak, swallowed, and tried once more. "We got our hearts set on her," he faltered.

Grandpa pushed his battered hat to one side and scratched his head. "All right, boy," he sighed. "The stall is yours."

A moment later Paul was telling Maureen the good news. "Owning a stall is next best to owning a pony," she laughed, as they both went to work in a fever of excitement.

With long brooms and steaming pails of water, they washed the walls and the ceiling of Phantom's stall. They scraped inches of sand from the hard-packed floor, dumped it in the woods, and brought in fresh, clean sand. They built a manger, spending long moments deciding just how high it should be placed. They scrubbed a rain barrel to be used for a

watering trough. They even dug a "wickie"—the long, tough root of a brier that trails along under the ground.

"Phantom won't be frightened when she smells and feels a wickie halter," Maureen said. "It'll be much softer than rope."

Chapter 6

PONY PENNING DAY

PONY PENNING DAY always comes on the last Thursday in July. For weeks before, every member of the Volunteer Fire Department is busy getting the grounds in readiness, and the boys are allowed to help.

"I'll do your chores at home, Paul," offered Maureen, "so's you can see that the pony pens are good and stout."

Paul spent long days at the pony penning grounds. Yet he could not have told how or by whom the tents were rigged up. He hardly noticed when the chutes for the bronco busting were built. He did not know who pounded the race track into condition. All he knew was that the pens for the wild ponies must be made fast. Once the Phantom was captured, she must not escape. Nothing else mattered.

The night before the roundup, he and Maureen made last-minute plans in Phantom's stall. "First thing in the morning," Paul told Maureen, "you lay a clean bed of dried sea grass. Then fill the manger with plenty of marsh grass to make Phantom feel at home."

"Oh, I will, Paul. And I've got some ear corn and some 'lasses to coax her appetite, and Grandma gave me a bunch of tiny new carrots and some rutabagas, and I've been saving up sugar until I have a little sackful."

In the midst of their talk, Grandpa, looking as if he had a surprise, joined them.

"I hain't rode on a roundup to Assateague for two year," he smiled, hiding one hand behind his back, "but I recom-member we allus had a chaw and a goody after the ponies was rounded up and afore we swimmed 'em across the channel. Here, Paul," he said, with a strange huskiness, "here's a choclit bar fer ye to take along." And he pressed the slightly squashed candy into Paul's hand.

It was dark and still when Paul awoke the next morning. He lay quiet a moment, trying to gather his wits. Suddenly he shot out of bed.

Today was Pony Penning Day!

His clothes lay on the chair beside his bed. Hurriedly he pulled on his shirt and pants and thudded barefoot down to the kitchen where Grandma stood over the stove, frying ham and making coffee for him as if he were man-grown!

He flung out his chest, sniffing the rich smells, bursting with excitement.

Grandma glanced around proudly. "I picked the first ripe figs of the year fer ye," she exclaimed. "They're chuckful of goodness. Now sit down, Paul, and eat a breakfast fit for a roundup man!"

Paul sat on the edge of his chair. With one eye on the clock he tried to eat the delicious figs and ham, but the food seemed to lump in his throat. Luckily Grandpa and Maureen came downstairs just then and helped clean his plate when Grandma was busy testing her cornbread in the oven with a long wisp of straw.

"I got to go now," Paul swallowed, as he ran out the door. He mounted Watch Eyes, a dependable pony that Grandpa had never been able to sell because of his white eyes. Locking his bare feet around the pony's sides, he jogged out of the yard.

Maureen came running to see him off.

"Whatever happens," Paul called back over his shoulder, "you be at Old Dominion Point at ten o'clock on a fresh pony."

"I'll be there, Paul!"

"And you, Paul!" yelled Grandpa. "Obey yer leader. No matter what!"

Day was breaking. A light golden mist came up out of the sea. It touched the prim white houses and the white picket fences with an unearthly light. Paul loped along slowly to save his mount's strength. He studied each house with a new interest. Here lived the woman who paid Maureen three dollars for hoeing her potato patch. There lived Kim Horsepepper, the clamdigger they had worked for. Mr. Horsepepper was riding out of his lane now, catching up with Paul. All along the road, men were turning out of their gates.

"Where do you reckon you'll do most good, Bub?" taunted a lean sapling of a man who, on other days, was an oysterman. He guffawed loudly, then winked at the rest of the group.

Paul's hand tightened on the reins. "Reckon I'll do most good where the leader tells me to go," he said, blushing hotly.

The day promised to be sultry. The marsh grass that usually billowed and waved stood motionless. The water of Assateague Channel glared like quicksilver.

Now the cavalcade was thundering over a small bridge that linked Chincoteague Island to little Piney Island. At the far end of the bridge a scow with a rail fence around it stood at anchor.

In spite of light talk, the faces of the men were drawn tight with excitement as they led their mounts onto the scow. The horses felt the excitement, too. Their nostrils quivered, and their ears swiveled this way and that, listening to the throb of the motor. Now the scow began to nose its way across the narrow

61

channel. Paul watched the White Hills of Assateague loom
near. He watched the old lighthouse grow sharp and sharper
against the sky. In a few minutes the ride was over. The gang-
way was being lowered. The horses were clattering down, each
man taking his own.

All eyes were on Wyle Maddox, the leader.

"Split in three bunches," Wyle clipped out the directions
loud and sharp. "North, south, and east. Me and Kim and
the Beebe boy will head east, Wimbrow and Quillen goes
north, and Harvey and Rodgers south. We'll all meet at
Tom's Point."

At the first sound of Wyle's steam-whistle voice, the sea birds rose with a wild clatter.

"They're like scouts," Paul said to himself. "They're going to warn the wild ponies that the enemy has landed."

"Gee-up!" shouted Wyle as he whirled his horse and motioned Kim and Paul to follow.

Paul touched his bare heels into Watch Eye's side. *They were off!* The boy's eyes were fastened on Wyle Maddox. He and Kim Horsepepper were following their leader like the wake of a ship.

As they rode on, Paul could feel the soft sand give way to hard meadowland, then to pine-laden trails. There were no paths to follow, only openings to skin through—openings that led to water holes or to grazing grounds. The three horses thrashed through underbrush, jumped fallen trees, waded brack-ish pools and narrow, winding streams.

Suddenly Paul saw Wyle Maddox' horse rear into the air. He heard him neigh loudly as a band of wild ponies darted into an open grazing stretch some twenty yards ahead, then vanished among the black tree trunks.

The woods came alive with thundering hooves and frantic horse calls. Through bush and brier and bog and hard marshland the wild ponies flew. Behind them galloped the three riders, whooping at the top of their lungs. For whole seconds at a time the wild band would be swallowed up by the forest gloom. Then it would reappear far ahead—nothing but a flash of flying tails and manes.

Suddenly Wyle Maddox was waving Paul to ride close. "A straggler!" he shouted, pointing off to the left. "He went that-a-way! Git him!" And with a burst of speed Wyle Maddox and Kim Horsepepper were after the band.

Paul was alone. His face reddened with anger. They wanted to be rid of him. That's what they wanted. Sent after a straggler! He was not interested in rounding up a straggler that couldn't even keep up with the herd! He wanted the Phantom. Then Grandpa's words flashed across his mind. "Obey yer leader. No matter what!"

He wheeled his pony and headed blindly in the direction Wyle had indicated. He rode deeper into the pine thicket, trying to avoid snapping twigs, yet watching ahead for the slightest motion of leaf or bush. He'd show the men, if it took him all day! His thin shirt clung to him damply and his body was wet with sweat. A cobweb veiled itself across his face. With one hand he tried to wipe it off, but suddenly he was almost unseated. Watch Eyes was dancing on his hind legs, his nose high in the air. Paul stared into the sun-dappled forest until his eyes burned in his head. At last, far away and deep in the shadow of the pines, he saw a blur of motion. With the distance that lay between them, it might have been anything. A deer. Or even a squirrel. Whatever it was, he was after it!

Watch Eyes plunged on. There was a kind of glory in pursuit that made Paul and the horse one. They were trailing nothing but swaying bushes. They were giving chase to a mirage. Always it moved on and on, showing itself only in quivering leaves or moving shadows.

What was that? In the clump of myrtle bushes just ahead? Paul reined in. He could scarcely breathe for the wild beating of his heart. There it was again! A silver flash. It looked like mist with the sun on it. And just beyond the mist, he caught sight of a long tail of mingled copper and silver.

He gazed awestruck. "It could be the Phantom's tail," he breathed. "It is! It is! It is! And the silver flash—it's not mist at all, but a brand-new colt, too little to keep up with the band."

The blood pounded in his ears. No wonder the Phantom was a straggler! No wonder she let herself be caught. "She's got a baby colt!" he murmured.

He glanced about him helplessly. If only he could think! How could he drive the Phantom and her colt to Tom's Point?

Warily he approached the myrtle thicket, then stopped as a hot wave of guilt swept over him. Phantom and her colt did not want to be rounded up by men. He could set them

free. No one had brought the Phantom in before. No one need ever know.

Just then the colt let out a high, frightened whinny. In that little second Paul knew that he wanted more than anything in the world to keep the mother and the colt together. Shivers of joy raced up and down his spine. His breath came faster. He made a firm resolution. "I'll buy you both!" he promised.

But how far had he come? Was it ten miles to Tom's Point or two? Would it be best to drive them down the beach? Or through the woods? As if in answer a loud bugle rang through the woods. It was the Pied Piper! And unmistakably his voice came from the direction of Tom's Point.

The Phantom pricked her ears. She wheeled around and almost collided with Watch Eyes in her haste to find the band. She wanted the Pied Piper for protection. Behind her trotted the foal, all shining and clean with its newness.

Paul laughed weakly. *He* was not driving the Phantom after all! She and her colt were leading him. They were leading him to Tom's Point!

Chapter 7

SHE CAN'T TURN BACK

TOM'S POINT was a protected piece of land where the
marsh was hard and the grass especially sweet. About seventy
wild ponies, exhausted by their morning's run, stood browsing
quietly, as if they were in a corral. Only occasionally they
looked up at their captors. The good meadow and their own
weariness kept them peaceful prisoners.

At a watchful distance the roundup men rested their
mounts and relaxed. It was like the lull in the midst of a storm.
All was quiet on the surface. Yet there was an undercurrent
of tension. You could tell it in the narrowed eyes of the men,

their subdued voices and their too easy laughter.

Suddenly the laughter stilled. Mouths gaped in disbelief. Eyes rounded. For a few seconds no one spoke at all. Then a shout that was half wonder and half admiration went up from the men. Paul Beebe was bringing in *the Phantom and a colt!*

Even the wild herds grew excited. As one horse, they stopped grazing. Every head jerked high, to see and to smell the newcomers. The Pied Piper whirled out and gathered the mare and her colt into his band. He sniffed them all over as if to make sure that nothing had harmed them. Then he snorted at Phantom, as much as to say, "You cause me more trouble than all the rest of my mares put together!"

The roundup men were swarming around Paul, buzzing with questions.

"How'd you *do* it, Paul?" Wyle Maddox called over the excited hubbub.

"Where'd you find 'em?" shouted Kim Horsepepper.

Paul made no answer. The questions floated around and above him like voices in a dream. He went hot and cold by turns. Did he do the right thing by bringing the Phantom and her foal in? Miserably he watched the Phantom's head droop. There was no wild sweep to her mane and her tail now. The free wild thing was caught like a butterfly in a net. She was webbed in by men, yelling and laughing.

"Beats all!" he heard someone say. "For two years we been trying to round up the Phantom and along comes a spindling youngster to show us up."

"'Twas the little colt that hindered her."

"'Course it was."

"It's the newest colt in the bunch; may not stand the swim."

"If we lose only one colt, it'll still be a good day's work."

"Jumpin' Jupiter, but it's hot!"

The men accepted Paul as one of them now—a real roundup man. They were clapping him on the shoulder and offering him candy bars. Suddenly he remembered the bar

Grandpa had pressed into his hand. He took off the wrapper and ate—not because he was hungry, but because he wanted to seem one of the men. They were trying to get him to talk. "Ain't they a shaggy-lookin' bunch?" Kim Horsepepper asked.

"Except for Misty," Paul said, pointing toward the Phantom's colt. "Her coat is silky." The mere thought of touching it sent shivers through him. "Misty," he thought to himself wonderingly. "Why, I've named her!"

The little foal was nursing greedily. Paul's eyes never strayed from the two of them. It was as if they might disappear into the mist of the morning, leaving only the sorrels and the bays and the blacks behind.

Only once he looked out across the water. Two lines of boats were forming a pony-way across the channel. He saw the cluster of people and the mounts waiting on the shores of Chincoteague and he knew that somewhere among them was Maureen. It was like a relay race. Soon she would carry on.

"Could I swim my mount across the channel alongside the Phantom?" Paul asked Wyle Maddox anxiously.

Wyle shook his head. "Watch Eyes is all tuckered out," he said. "Besides, there's a kind of tradition in the way things is handled on Pony Penning Day. There's mounted men for the roundup and there's boatmen to herd 'em across the channel," he explained.

"Tide's out!" he called in clipped tones. "Current is slack. Time for the ponies to be swimmed across. Let's go!"

72

Suddenly the beach was wild with commotion. From three sides the roundup men came rushing at the ponies, their hoarse cries whipping the animals into action. They plunged into the water, the stallions leading, the mares following, neighing encouragement to their colts.

"They're off!" shouted Wyle Maddox, and everyone felt the relief and triumph in his words.

Kim thumped Paul on the back as they boarded the scow for the ride back. "Don't fret about yer prize," he said brusquely. "You've got the Phantom sure this time. Once in the water she can't turn back."

But he was wrong!

Chapter 8

CAUGHT IN THE WHIRLPOOL

ON THE shores of Chincoteague the people pressed forward, their faces strained to stiffness, as they watched Assateague Beach.

"Here they come!" The cry broke out from every throat.

Maureen, wedged in between Grandpa Beebe on one side and a volunteer fireman on the other, stood on her mount's back. Her arms paddled the air as if she were swimming and struggling with the wild ponies.

Suddenly a fisherman, looking through binoculars, began shouting in a hoarse voice, "A new-borned colt is afeared to

74

swim! It's knee-deep in the water, and won't go no further."

The crowds yelled their advice. "What's the matter with the roundup men?" "Why don't they heft it into deep water—it'll swim all right!" "Why don't they hist it on the scow?"

The fisherman was trying to get a better view. He was crawling out over the water on a wall of piling. It seemed a long time before he put his binoculars to his eyes again. The people waited breathlessly. A small boy began crying.

"Sh!" quieted his mother. "Listen to the man with the four eyes."

"The colt's too little to swim," the fisherman bawled out. "Wait! A wild pony is breaking out from the mob. Swimming around the mob! Escaping!"

An awed murmur stirred the crowds. Maureen dug her toes in her mount's back. She strained her eyes to see the fugitive, but all she could make out was a milling mass of dark blobs on the water.

The fisherman leaned far out over the water. He made a megaphone of one hand. "Them addle-brained boatmen can't stop the pony," his voice rasped. "It's outsmarting 'em all."

Maureen's mind raced back to other Pony Pennings. The Phantom upsetting a boat. The Phantom fleeing through the woods. Always escaping. Always free. She clutched the neck of her blouse. She felt gaspy, like a fish flapping about on dry land. Why was the man with the binoculars so slow? Why didn't he say, "It's the Phantom!" Who else could it be?

Now he was waving one arm wildly. He looked like a straw in the wind. He teetered. He lost his balance. He almost fell into the water in his excitement.

"It's the Phantom!" he screamed at last. "I can see the white map on her shoulders!"

The people took up the cry, echoing it over and over. "It's the Phantom! She's escaped again!"

Maureen felt tears on her cheek, and impatiently brushed them away.

Again the fisherman was waving for quiet.

"Hush!" bellowed Grandpa Beebe.

The people fell silent. They were like listeners around a microphone. "It's the *Phantom's* colt that won't swim!" he called out in a voice so hoarse it cracked. "The Phantom got separated from a bran'-fire new colt. She's gone back to get it!"

The people whooped and hollered at the news. "The Phantom's got a colt," they sang out. "The Phantom's got a new colt!"

Again the fisherman was waving for silence.

"She's reached her colt!" he crowed. "But the roundup men are closing in on her! They're making her shove the colt in the water. She's makin' it swim!"

Grandpa Beebe cupped his hands around his mouth. "Can the little feller make it?" he boomed.

The crowd stilled, waiting for the hoarse voice. For long seconds no answer came. The fisherman remained as fixed as the piling he stood on. Wave after wave of fear swept over Maureen. She felt as if she were drowning. And just when she could stand the silence no longer, the fisherman began reporting in short, nervous sentences.

"They're half-ways across. Jumpin' Jupiter! The colt! It's bein' sucked down in a whirlpool. I can't see it now. My soul and body! A boy's jumped off the scow. He's swimming out to help the colt."

The onlookers did not need the fisherman with the binoculars any more. They could see for themselves. A boy swimming against the current. A boy holding a colt's head above the swirling water.

Maureen gulped great lungfuls of air. "It's Paul!" she screamed. "It's Paul!"

On all sides the shouts went up. "Why, it's Paul!"

"Paul Beebe!"

Grandpa leaped up on his mount's back as nimbly as a boy. He stood with his arms upraised, his fists clenched.

"God help ye, Paul!" his words carried out over the water. "Yer almost home!"

Grandpa's voice was as strong as a tow rope. Paul was swimming steadily toward it, holding the small silver face of the colt above the water. He was almost there. He *was* there!

Maureen slid down from her mount, clutching a handful of mane. "You made it, Paul! You made it!" she cried.

The air was wild with whinnies and snorts as the ponies touched the hard sand, then scrambled up the shore, their wet bodies gleaming in the sun. Paul half-carried the little colt up the steep bank; then suddenly it found its own legs.

Shouts between triumph and relief escaped every throat as the little filly tottered up the bank. Almost to the top, her feet went scooting out from under her and she was down on the sand, her sides heaving.

Maureen felt a new stab of fear.

If only the big ponies would not crush her! That tender white body among all those thrashing hooves. What chance had she? What chance with the wild wind for a mother?

But all the wildness seemed to have ebbed out of the Phantom. She picked her forefeet high. Then she carefully straddled her colt, and fenced in the small white body with her own slender legs.

For a brief second Paul's and Maureen's eyes met above the crowds. It was as if they and the mare and her foal were the only creatures on the island. They were unaware of the great jostling and fighting as the stallions sorted out their own mares and colts. They were unaware of everything but a sharp ecstasy. Soon the Phantom and her colt would belong to them. Never to be sold.

The Pied Piper wheeled around Paul. He peered at the dripping boy from under his matted forelock. Then he trumpeted as if to say: "This sopping creature is no mare of mine!"

And he pushed Paul out of the way while the crowds laughed hysterically.

Dodging horses and people, Grandpa Beebe made his way over to Paul.

"Paul, boy," he said, his voice unsteady, "I swimmed the hull way with you. Yer the most wonderful and the craziest young'un in the world. Now git home right smart quick," he added, trying to sound very stern. "Yer about done up, and Grandma's expectin' ye. Maureen and I'll see to it that the Phantom and her colt reach the pony pens."

Chapter 9

ON TO THE PONY PENNING GROUNDS

IT WAS NOW mid-morning and the hot July sun was high in the heavens. The wild ponies stood with heads hanging low, tails tucked in. They looked beaten and confused. Only the Phantom's foal seemed contented. She slept, her sides rising and falling in the cool shade made by the mare's body.

"Rest 'em a bit longer," Wyle Maddox directed. "Then on to the pony pens."

Maureen sat watching, thinking. The little colt must never know the hungry feeling of being without a mother. But the hundred dollars? Would it pay for both?

She was jolted out of her thoughts with the cry, "Get-a-going!"

Onlookers fell back while Maureen, Grandpa Beebe, and the other horsemen surrounded the ponies and began driving them toward town. The Phantom broke at the start, her colt weaving along behind her like the tail of a kite.

"Please, God, don't let Phantom escape now!" breathed Maureen as she and Grandpa Beebe took out after them. But Phantom could not travel fast with her stilty-legged youngster. Maureen soon came upon them, hidden among the foliage of a kinksbush, the Phantom's proud, wild face and the colt's

comical baby face all framed round with green leaves.

With a shout she drove them back into the herd.

After that the mare no longer tried to escape, for there were no openings into the cool woods—only lines of cars and visitors forming a solid fence on either side of them.

Slowly and dejectedly the wild ponies paraded through the main streets of Chincoteague. Only the Phantom's colt seemed happy with her lot. She could smell her dam close by. Her stomach was stretched tight with milk. She was full of sleep. She kicked her heels sideways, dancing along, letting out little whinnies of joy. She seemed to *like* Chincoteague.

All up and down the streets the people came spilling out of their houses, shouting to one another as they recognized some mare or stallion from previous roundups.

"There's that pinto with the shark eyes."

"Look at the Pied Piper! His forelock's grown 'most as long as his tail!"

"See all the big colts!"

"Who's the chestnut mare with the white mark on her shoulders?"

"Not the Phantom! Not her!" they gasped in disbelief.

"It *is* the Phantom!" someone yelled in answer. "And she's got a colt! I saw 'em swim in!"

"And Paul Beebe caught her," someone else called. "I heard Kim Horsepepper tell all about it."

The excitement ran from house to house like a flame in the wind. "They got the Phantom! Paul Beebe got her! And she's leadin' a colt!"

Through the shouting, elbowing crowd, the slow parade went on—past stores and restaurants, past the white frame hotel, past the red brick firehouse which the colts of other years had paid for.

Maureen looked straight ahead. She stayed so close to the Phantom and her foal that when the foal looked sideways Maureen could see her long golden eyelashes.

At last the procession turned into the pony penning grounds. It moved quickly once around the ring. Then once

again, while children and parents and horse dealers hung over the fence. The children shouted at the top of their lungs.

"Oh, Dad! Buy me that colt with the star on her face!"

"I want the one with the white stockings!"

"I want the littlest one!"

Only the dealers were silent. They were thinking in terms of buying and selling.

Grandpa Beebe rode close to Maureen. "We got 'em here," he sighed sharply. "Now it's up to the men afoot."

Again that feeling of something pressing against her throat came to Maureen as she watched the men on foot drive the ponies out of the ring, separating the colts from their mothers. They herded the colts into small pens, giving the mares and stallions the run of a big corral.

Suddenly it was the Phantom's turn to be herded into the corral. She flew ahead of the men, never allowing them to touch her. Now two brawny men were making a grab for her foal. For long seconds the men held the foal high, their hands supporting her little round belly. Then they put her down, slapped her hip and sent her along with her dam into the big corral.

Maureen drew a deep breath of happiness. "The colt's too little to leave her mother. Too little!" she whispered into Grandpa's whiskery ear. "They'll let them stay together."

Then she hurried home to tell Paul.

"Paul's asleep," Grandma said, "and you leave him be. I got some butter beans warmin' fer ye and some nice fresh cornbread sittin' a-top the oven."

While Maureen ate, Grandma talked on. "I kin see you're boilin' over with things to tell, but they'll keep till you've ate. Between whiles I'll do the talkin'." She closed one eye in thought. "Let's see. Oh, Victoria Pruitt stopped by. Figgered you or Paul might like to earn some money helpin' her and Mr. Pruitt catch chickens. They're fixin' to ship 'em to Norfolk. But I told Mis' Victoria yer money pouch was fat as a tick."

Maureen's spoon fell to the floor.

"Oh, Grandma! The Phantom's got a colt and we got to earn a lot of money to buy her, too."

Grandma looked at Maureen's plate. She saw that the beans were gone and there was nothing left of the cornbread but a few crumbs. "Go 'long," she nodded. "Mis' Victoria wanted ye right much."

Maureen spent the afternoon chasing hundreds of chickens and cooping them up in little crates. By sundown her arms were pecked and scratched and her face streaked with perspiration.

As she walked home, clutching two dollars in her moist hand, she saw Paul riding toward her on Watch Eyes.

"Leg up behind me," he called out. "I got to go to the store for Grandma. You can help carry the things."

Maureen scrambled up behind her brother. "Paul!"

"Huh?"

"Do you reckon the firemen'll sell us both the Phantom and the little one?"

"'Course. The colt's too young to take away from the mare."

"But where'll we get the money?"

Paul slowed Watch Eyes to a walk. "I been working on it whilst I slept," he said. "What time does the sale begin?"

"It says half-past nine on the program."

"All right," exclaimed Paul, giving Watch Eyes his head "You and I'll get to the pony penning grounds at sunup. We'll wait there at the entrance for the fire chief. Soon as he comes, we'll say to him: 'We got exactly one hundred dollars, sir. We earned it in less'n four months. In four months more we can earn another hundred. Y'see, chief, we're fixin' to buy the Phantom—and Misty, too.'"

"Why, Paul! That's *exactly* what we'll do. It'll be just as easy as that." She threw her arms about Paul's waist. "Misty," she chuckled. "Who named the Phantom's colt?"

"She kind of named herself," Paul answered. "When I was in the woods there on Assateague, I couldn't tell if I was seeing white mist with the sun on it, or a live colt. The minute I knew 'twas a live colt, I kept calling her Misty in my mind."

"Misty!" said Maureen softly. "Misty," she repeated as they jogged along. "She came up out of the sea."

Grandpa was in the kitchen, standing before a mirror, trimming the bristles in his ears when Maureen and Paul came in with the groceries.

"Consarn it all!" he fussed. "Do you got to rustle them bags like cows trompin' through a cornfield? A fella can't hear his-self think, let alone hold his hand steady. This here's a mighty ticklish job."

"Why, Clarence!" exclaimed Grandma, "I've never seed you so twittery."

"Ef'n you had whiskbrooms in your ears, maybe you'd be twittery, too."

Grandma stopped basting the marsh hen she had just taken out of the oven and burst out in helpless laughter. "Whiskbrooms in my ears!" she chortled. And soon Maureen and Paul and even Grandpa were laughing with her.

"All right now," said Grandma, recovering her breath. "Maureen, you can set the potatoes to boil and lay the table. Lay an extra place like allus. Never know when some human straggler is goin' to stop. And bein' as it's Pony Penning Day you kin cut a few of them purty-by-nights and some bouncin' Bess fer a centerpiece."

No straggler came. Just the four of them sat around the table while a light wind played with the curtains. Grandpa became more like himself with each mouthful of the tender marsh hen.

"The reason I was jumpy," he confessed, "was account of thinkin' about that Phantom you children wanter buy. No one of sound mind ever buys a three-year-old wild pony. Why, Phantom's like the topsail on a ship—a moon-raker she is!"

The flapping of the curtain broke the little pause that followed.

"Besides," Grandpa continued, "My feet is killin' me. Reckon we're in fer a blow. A sou'wester come up this afternoon, and I never seed a nor'easter take no back talk from a sou'wester."

"If a thunder squall's a-brewin'," spoke Grandma, "the children got to stay home from the race tonight."

Paul's and Maureen's eyes sought Grandpa's, as much as to say, "How can you do this to us? Why, the race on the eve of the sale is almost as important as the roundup!"

"Oh," coughed Grandpa, "it'll be *after* the race afore the weather turns squally. And my advice is fer the children to go right smart quick so they kin mill around in the colt pens afore the race. They might find a critter with lots purtier markings than the Phantom."

Paul and Maureen leaped to their feet. They galloped around and around the table, stopping to nose Grandma and Grandpa like curious colts. Then they soberly promised to visit the colt pens, but in their hearts they knew there was room only for the Phantom and Misty.

Chapter 10

COLTS HAVE GOT TO GROW UP

AS PAUL and Maureen stood inside the big corral, looking at Misty, they knew she was the finest-blooded foal in the world. Oh, the beauty of her! She was neither silver nor gold. She was both. And she had a funny white blaze that started down the left side of her face, then did a right-about and covered her whole muzzle. It gave her a look of wonderment and surprise. Like her mother she, too, wore a white map of the United States on her withers, but the outlines were softer and blended into the gold of her body.

They could have gazed at her forever, exclaiming over her gold eyelashes, her pink underlip, her funny knobby knees, her short flappy tail, the furry insides of her ears. But suddenly Paul was aware of an uneasy feeling, as though someone were eying him. Then he felt a hot breath on the back of his neck. Slowly he turned his head and came face to face with the Pied Piper.

For an instant neither the stallion nor the boy winked an eyelash. Pied Piper stared fixedly at Paul from under his long forelock. He was like a man peering out from ambush. Paul could see the white ring around the stallion's eyes, the red lining of his nostrils, the ears flattened. He could smell the wildness. He sensed that one false move, and a darting foreleg might knock him down as if he were a cornstalk. He opened his mouth to speak, but for a long time no sound came.

"Your baby," he spoke at last in the softest of voices, "your baby is—is beautiful."

The Pied Piper's ears twitched ever so slightly.

"You mean *our* filly!" corrected Maureen in her strong, high voice.

The Pied Piper laced his ears back again. He bared his teeth, breathing loudly.

"I'm not talking to you, Maureen," Paul whispered, his face pale. "Turn your head."

The Pied Piper's ears pricked once more. That curious soft voice!

"Oh," Maureen breathed, as she caught sight of the stallion. "Your baby is beautiful," she gasped. "And so is your mare."

"So are all your mares," added Paul for good measure. "Excuse us, sir, but we must see the race now." He and Maureen began backing slowly toward the fence.

Just then a stallion from another band came over to study the Pied Piper's family. The Pied Piper forgot Paul and

Maureen in the more important business of bunching his mares behind him.

"Whew!" said Paul breathlessly, as they scrambled over the fence, "that was a close one."

On the way to the race track they had to pass between the colt pens.

"We almost forgot our promise to look at the colts!" they both exclaimed in the same breath.

Hurriedly they squeezed in between the spectators and perched on the top rail of one of the pens. Their faces paled as they looked down.

Round and round the pen the colts were plodding, searching for their mothers, flinging their heads up, whimpering, trying to suckle anything their muzzles could reach.

"Why, they're as close packed as oysters in a barrel!" exclaimed Paul.

"They're children, lost and scared," said Maureen. "Let's go!" she cried through white lips. "Let's go! I can't abide the nickerin'. The young things are hungry."

Paul felt as if he were going to be sick. "I can't abide it, either," he said. Then his mouth thinned to a line and he doubled his fists. "I'm going to see the fire chief about this!"

The fire chief was a big, broad-shouldered man who walked with a cane. There were times when the cane seemed to dangle uselessly in his hands. But when he was tired, he leaned on it heavily.

They found him now in the center of a group of visitors, both hands gripping his cane. His face was sun-blistered and weary, but his eyes lighted when he saw Paul and Maureen.

"Here's Paul Beebe, the lad who swam the colt ashore," he explained to the little group. "And his sister, Maureen, who . . ."

The crowd shifted, began surrounding Paul, pelting questions at him. "Did the colt try to drag you down like a drowning person?" "How old is it?" "How wide is the channel where you swam across?"

Paul and Maureen scarcely heard the questions.

"What are you two looking so hollow-eyed about?" the chief asked as he drew the children aside.

"It's about the colts," Maureen stammered.

"Yes," said Paul. "We don't believe they should be taken from their mothers, and we aim to do something about it— if you'll let us, sir. We got lots of milk in the ice chest at home, and once we raised up a foal on a big nursing bottle and we still got the bottle. It's cruel to starve the young things."

The fire chief stood silent and thoughtful. He looked past the grounds and out to the bay, where the masts of the fishing boats formed spider-thin lines against the graying sky.

"I don't know if I can make you understand about this, but I'll try," he began slowly. "Colts have got to grow up sometime. Their mothers can't go on babying them all their lives. Haven't you two seen a mare tell her youngster to rustle his own living?"

Paul and Maureen nodded in silence.

"She can't tell the colt in so many words," the fire chief continued. "She just kicks him away. Gentle-like at first. Then good and hard if he won't understand. Sometimes she has to get pretty rough, especially when she's going to have a new foal in a few months."

"But those little colts . . ."

"Those little fellows," nodded the chief, "are old enough to fend for themselves. Separating them from their mothers is the kindest way we know to teach them how."

Paul and Maureen reddened. They felt very young and foolish as they thanked the fire chief for explaining things.

"Don't thank me, you two. When I was rising up atwixt a youngster and a grownup, the same question worried me every Pony Penning Day. Finally, I watched a mare tell her colt to grow up and then I quit worrying. Now I want you to quit worrying, too.

"Besides," he added as he pulled out his watch, "it's almost time for the race. Black Comet will be running any minute now. It's high time," he said, tapping his cane in the sawdust, "it's high time we islanders raised up a competitor for Black Comet. Things have been much too easy for him."

"Tell him now," nudged Maureen, her eyes shining.

"Chief!" said Paul, trying to make his voice behave. "Next year Black Comet will have a *real* competitor. Maureen and I want to buy the Phant—"

But the fire chief never heard what Paul had to say. His words were drowned by a voice blaring over the loud speaker.

"Tonight, ladies and gentlemen, Black Comet from Pocomoke is racing against Patches and Lucy Lee of Chincoteague."

Chapter 11

STORM-SHY

FEELING much happier, Paul and Maureen joined the throngs hurrying to see Black Comet. Black Comet was five years old. For three of those years he had been brought over from Pocomoke on the mainland to race for the Pony Penning crowds on the eve of the sale. And for three years he had won. Twice he led by several lengths, and once he led only by a nose. But always he won.

This night was no different. Black Comet pranced to the starting line, sure of himself. His jockey, too, was sure. They both seemed bored with the excited antics of the two other entries. One was a flashy black-and-white pony named Patches. He danced on his hind feet, bolted past the starting line, and had to be brought back again and again. The other entry was Lucy Lee, a nervous little mare.

Black Comet threw back his head and let out a high horse laugh at them as if to say, "You're wasting your time."

And they were! The race belonged to Black Comet from the start. He broke out in front and stayed there.

Maureen beat her fists on the fence rail. "Come on, Patches! Come on, Lucy Lee! Don't let Black Comet win every time!"

"Next year the Phantom will be in there!" Paul kept saying. "Next year the Phantom."

Just as Black Comet crossed the finish line, a bolt of lightning split the sky.

At that same instant Paul felt a strong hand grip his shoulder. It was Grandpa Beebe. His face was spattered with dirt and his clean blue shirt in ribbons.

"The squall ain't a promise no more," he shouted against the rising wind, "it's here! Paul, you stay and help the fire chief. Maureen, you come home with me.

"And Paul! If the storm gits too heavy," he called back over his shoulder, "you take shelter in our truck. It's backed up nigh to the colt pens."

The grounds burst into noise and confusion. The wind whined. It caught at the tent flaps, snapping them like whips.

White paper programs spiraled through the air, driven first one way, then the other. Children, over-tired and frightened, cried to be taken home. Thunder rumbled deep out of the heavens. Colts in their pens squealed. Stallions trumpeted.

Paul fought his way to the pony pens, dodging people, dodging pieces of paper which the wind swept into his face. He could scarcely see his way. The strings of colored electric bulbs waved back and forth, throwing weird shadows.

At last he came upon the fire chief, brandishing his cane and shouting directions: "Dan, you do this! Joe, you do that! Paul . . ."

Paul strained his ears to hear, but suddenly the skies seemed to open and rain fell in great torrents. The swaying lights went out, plunging the island into darkness.

"Everyone go home!" called the chief. "Nothing we can do now." A flash of lightning showed him limping toward his car.

Paul did not follow. The rain beat down on him fiercely. It felt cold and hard, like gunshot. How could Misty stand it? "She's so little," he thought. "She's bound to be storm-shy. I know what I'll do! I'll carry her to the truck and shelter her until the storm is past."

Warmed by his decision, he ran past the colt pens and on to the big corral. Lightning sizzled across the sky, flooding the earth with an eerie white. It showed the wild ponies, separated into four bands. Paul's eyes leaped from one band to another, trying to find the Pied Piper's family, but darkness

closed in. He held his breath, waiting for another flash. It came. It picked out the stallion's creamy-white mane.

Quickly Paul scrambled over the fence. He waited again, his eyes fastened on the spot where the Pied Piper's band stood huddled. He held onto the fence with one hand and made a watershed over his eyes with the other. He waited again for the lightning. It came tearing across the sky. He could see the Pied Piper's family as plainly as if it were daylight, but the Phantom and Misty were not among them. They were gone! Stolen! Some other stallion had stolen them! The thought flashed through his mind.

Shivering and drenched, he ran from one band to the other. He stumbled over tree stumps and fell flat in the water. His mouth was gritty with sand and mud. He went on blindly, feeling every hump in the grass, every fallen log; but nowhere in all that big corral could he find the tiny foal or her wild dam.

Running, slipping, falling, running, he made his way to the pony trucks. Most of the trucks were empty, waiting for tomorrow's sale. A few held a colt or two—big colts, big and shaggy.

Sick with fear for Phantom and Misty, he sought the shelter of Grandpa Beebe's truck to think out where they might be. Could Phantom have leaped the fence? Could Misty have rolled out under it? He stopped short. There, in the body of the truck, under a piece of tarpaulin, he felt rather than saw a slight stirring. He trembled, not from cold, but from fear that what he prayed was a mare and her colt would turn out instead to be bags of feed. He cried out for a flash of lightning. It came in a streak, filling the truck with yellow light. And in that split second Paul saw the Phantom and Misty, their heads lowered in a corner like children being punished at school.

He threw back his head for joy and let the rain beat on his face. So that was why Grandpa's shirt was torn and his face seamed with dirt! He had brought them to shelter before the storm broke.

Paul opened the door of the cab, half expecting Grandpa to be there. It was empty—except for Grandpa's old rain jacket that lay on the seat, and the strong smell of tobacco. He ripped off his wet shirt, his denim pants. His teeth chattered as he pulled on the warm, dry jacket. It was so long it almost covered his underwear. He ran around to the tailgate of the truck and steadied himself on the spare tire. Slowly, cautiously, hardly daring to breathe, he climbed up and over the tailgate and into the truck.

The storm blotted out any sound he might have made. But the Phantom sensed his presence. She neighed sharply to Misty, who caught her fear. Paul could hear the small rat-a-tat of her hooves.

He leaned hard against the stakes of the truck, every muscle tensed. Phantom would either charge him or stay as far away as possible. He waited, counting the seconds. He could hear the rain sloshing over the tarpaulin, spilling down the sides of

the truck. He could smell the steamy warmth of furry bodies. He could smell the sea. And in the occasional flashes of light,

he saw the copper-and-white tail of the Phantom sweeping nervously over Misty. Paul let out a deep sigh of relief. She was *not* going to charge him.

He never knew how long he stood there. He only knew that after awhile the Phantom no longer mistrusted him. She seemed to doze off for seconds at a time, as if she felt a oneness with him; as if she and her foal and this shivering, wet boy were fellow creatures caught in a storm, prisoners of the elements. Prisoners together.

Together! The word sounded a bugle in Paul. Time stood still. There was only the wind and the rain and the three creatures together! Together!

Aching to reach out and touch first the shaggy coat, then the silky one, he plunged his hands deep into Grandpa's pockets to stay the impulse. His fingers felt a firm, slightly sticky object. He squeezed it. He traced a few dried stems, then paper-thin leaves pressed solidly together. It was a twist of chewing tobacco! Quickly he pulled it out of his pocket. The spicy sweetness of molasses filled his nostrils. He took long, deep breaths of it. His mind was turning somersaults. Molasses! Molasses! How ponies love it! Often he had seen Grandpa cut a quid for Watch Eyes. With trembling fingers he broke off a sizable piece and held it on his outstretched hand.

For a long time he waited. When he could stand no longer, he sank down on the cold, wet floor of the truck, still holding his hand toward the Phantom.

He waited, motionless.

He listened to the storm bell tolling out in the bay, and to the rain swishing and swirling around him. He felt little rivulets of perspiration run down his back. He grew hot and chilled by turns. His arm grew numb, then began to prickle as if hundreds of red-hot needles were jabbing him. His head reeled. It ached for lack of sleep.

And just when his hand was about to drop, he heard slow, questioning hooves placed one at a time on the floor of the truck. One step forward. Then a long pause filled in by the sobbing of the wind. Then another step. And another. Now a breath on his hand, now feelers sending chills of excitement up his arm, racing through his whole body. Now a soft muzzle lipping his palm. The tobacco gone! Lifted out of his hand by a pony so wild that she had upset a boat, so wild that for two years no one had caught her. A wild thing eating out of his hand! He wriggled his fingers in wonderment. All the numbness had gone out of them. He was not even trembling! Only this sharp ecstasy, this feeling that all of life was worth this moment. The roundup, the discovery of Misty, the swim across the channel—they all melted into this.

The moments rushed on. The storm quieted. Paul could hear the Phantom mouthing the tobacco. He tried to keep awake to enjoy the pleasant, soothing sound, but his eyes drooped. His breath steadied. He fell into a deep sleep, unmindful when the Phantom nosed him curiously from head to foot. Then she, too, began to doze.

At last Misty sank down in exhaustion. Her head fell across Paul's lap, not because she wanted human comfort, but because she was tired from the hard drive and the swim. The floor of a truck or a boy's lap were all the same to her, so long as her dam was near.

It was thus, at dawn, that Grandpa Beebe found them.

Chapter 12

THE SOLD ROPE

P AUL," whispered Grandpa in the low voice he used when children and wild animals were asleep. "Paul, boy . . ."

At sound of Grandpa's voice the Phantom neighed shrilly. Misty scrambled to her feet, swayed, then slid awkwardly along the floor of the truck. With a hungry little bleat, she found her mother's side and began nursing.

Paul opened his eyes, then quickly shut them. If this were a dream, he wanted to spin it out and make it last until the end of time. He wished Grandpa's voice would fade away, but it kept pricking him awake.

"Come, boy. Grandma is nigh crazy with worry over ye. The big pine tree fell atop the house last night and the Atlantic Ocean wetted our dooryard. I just couldn't come for ye till now."

Paul pulled himself up. His muscles ached. He could feel the wide stripes made by the boards of the truck across his back. He looked down at his long expanse of bare legs and suddenly remembered that he was wearing nothing but Grandpa's jacket over his underwear. He grinned at Grandpa.

Grandpa winked back. "I see you scamped my belongings," he chuckled. "It's any port in a storm, eh, lad?" Then he thought of his message. "Grandma's mixed some goose grease with onion syrup fer ye. Yer apt to catch a terrible fever," he quoted Grandma, but all the while his eyes were fondling the dam and her colt. "She says ye've got to come home and go to bed."

Paul felt the stickiness of his hand where the Phantom had nuzzled it. His voice tensed. "I can't leave, Grandpa. Today's the sale! We got to buy the Phantom and Misty."

"Maureen kin tend to that whilst ye get some sleep. I don't know what in thunderation made me protect that little feller fer ye last night. I must be getting addled in my old age. Now help me get the pair of 'em outen the truck and back in the corral so you can buy 'em legal-like at the sale."

But there was no need for help. With the truck backed up close to the corral gate, the Phantom flew down the ramp. She smelled the rain-washed grass. She was crazy to get to it. Misty followed, a silver fluff of a shadow.

The pony penning grounds were waking up when Maureen rode in on Watch Eyes. Volunteer firemen were clearing the damage done by the storm. Trucks bearing licenses from Maryland, New York, North Carolina, Washington, D. C., were beginning to line up close to the colt pens. A few children, their faces still flushed with sleep, darted here and there, talking to themselves: "That little black pony. I could name him Black Beauty!" "I want the one with the white stockings!"

"How-do, Maureen," called Tom, who on ordinary days was an oysterer. "Yer up and about mighty early. Reckon yer sharpenin' your appetite for the big dinner this noon! Or mebbe ye come to buy my last two chances on the sorrel pony bein' given away Saturday." And with a great flourish he whipped the tickets out of his pocket.

Maureen could think of no answer. She was not interested in the sorrel pony, and she had forgotten all about the dinner to be served in the big dining hall on the grounds. She managed to smile at Tom and thank him politely. Then feeling of the money pouch around her neck, and the piece of rope over her shoulder, she stated her business quickly. "I came to see the fire chief," she said.

"Nowheres about. He's been and gone."

"Oh!"

"Anything I can do?"

"Reckon not."

"Wal, he'll be back afore ye can say Chincoteague Isle."

Tying Watch Eyes to a tree, Maureen wandered about the grounds, waiting for the chief. She stopped at the colt pens and noticed that several of the shaggy-coated youngsters already wore sold ropes around their necks. She noticed, too, that most of them were beginning to eat for themselves. Only a few were whimpering for their mothers.

The fire chief was right, she thought. They're learning to be grownups.

She felt good toward the whole wide world as she walked toward the big corral. She watched two stallions fighting— dancing on their hind legs, lashing out with their forelegs. A news photographer was getting a picture of them. Finally she climbed the fence and jumped inside the corral.

The wild ponies were refreshed by the rain. They thundered past and around her. They paid her no more attention than if she had been a small tree. She was nothing but an obstacle to avoid. She stood listening to the wild music of their hooves. She liked to feel the little gusts of wind made by their flying bodies. She liked the sight of their manes and tails frisking with the wind.

The Pied Piper's band was on the far side of the corral. He was policing his family, keeping his mares in a bunch. Maureen saw Misty stretched out at her mother's feet.

Her heart warmed at sight of them. She walked over to them, slowly, slowly. If she could slip the sold rope over Misty's head, it would save all the struggle later. The firemen had no

time to "ease up" to the ponies. With a hundred or more colts to sell, they had to work fast. Often two men had to pick up a pony by its tail and its head in order to fasten a sold rope about its neck. Meanwhile, the pony screamed and fought and struggled to get away.

Probably it *doesn't* hurt, thought Maureen, but I'd like to save Misty all that scared feeling.

Suddenly her eyes flew wide with horror. The Phantom was tugging at a rope tied around Misty's neck. A sold rope! "No! No! No!" Maureen shrieked. "Phantom!" she cried hysterically, "you're the only one who can un-sell her. Try harder! Harder! Harder!"

Phantom was doing her best. With her big yellow teeth she was trying to sever the rope, but Misty would pull away,

thinking her mother was playing. She opened her little colt's mouth, biting back, neighing fiercely.

Maureen looked around helplessly. Just then she spied the fire chief coming toward the corral with Tom at his heels. She ran to them. "Misty's wearing a sold rope!" she cried. "Misty's been sold!" Then her voice failed her.

"*Who's* been sold?" asked the chief, puzzled.

"Who?" echoed Tom.

"Misty!" she choked, trying to swallow her tears.

The fire chief knotted his brows. "Now suppose you tell me who Misty is," he said kindly.

"Why, she's the Phantom's colt, and Paul and I—we've been saving for months to buy the Phantom, and now we want both her and her colt. And we have a hundred and two dollars," she added breathlessly as she patted the money around her neck, "right here in Grandpa's tobacco pouch. And in four months more we can save up another hundred. I can go clamming, and I can catch soft-shell crabs, and Paul can shuck oysters, and Uncle Ralph will give us his night catch of fatbacks, and Paul and I can go up and down the streets calling 'Fat-backs for sale, nice fresh fat-backs for sale!'"

"Well, why in thunder didn't you kids tell me!" exploded the fire chief. Then his voice quieted. "I'm sorry, Maureen. I didn't know. Why, less than an hour ago a man by the name of Foster came through on his way to Norfolk. Had business there, he said, and couldn't get back until after the sale. I asked Tom here to show him around and he took a fancy to the filly's markings."

"He bought Misty?"

"Paid fifty dollars down," nodded the chief. "Insisted on buying the Phantom, too, just so the colt'll get a good start in life." He took a deep breath. "Tom and I," he added, "tied the sold rope around the colt's neck, but it's going to take a lot more than two of us to handle that Phantom."

Maureen watched the sun slide out from behind a low cloud and make diamonds of the raindrops on the grass. She turned her back on it. How could the sun shine when things went wrong?

The fire chief clasped and unclasped his cane. "I had no idea," he spoke quietly. "If you had only said something about it yesterday."

Maureen was about to leave, but Tom called her back.

"How's about taking my last chances on the sorrel?" he suggested. "There's a *gentle* critter. And ye'd still have a hundred dollars to spend on candy and things."

Maureen raised her eyes to Tom's. Then she smiled at him through her tears. She felt sorry for Tom. Guess he's never really wanted anything, she thought, as she slowly walked over to untie Watch Eyes.

Chapter 13

A PONY CHANGES HANDS

PAUL took the news without a word, but all the sunburn suddenly washed out of his face, leaving it pinched and white.

The day passed in a kind of dream. Both Paul and Maureen tried to stay away from the grounds, but something drew them there. Yet they no longer belonged to the happy crowds. They were onlookers now, like hungry people on the outside of a restaurant window.

Sick with longing, they watched colts being tugged and pushed and lifted into waiting cars. Some went off in station wagons, some in trailers, some in dealers' trucks. Many of them squealed and kicked and fought. A few were too frightened to struggle.

They stared fixedly as Grandpa bought a truckload of yearlings. "Soon we'll be gentling them—for someone else," Maureen whispered sadly to Paul.

The day that was to be so full of excitement dragged out. Even the merry-go-round with its brightly painted ponies and its brassy music did not help them forget. To Paul, the music kept wheezing, "You found and lost Misty! You found and lost Misty! You found and lost Misty!" To Maureen it was a noisy mockery.

"We'll have us another hoss family. Just as purty. Mebbe purtier," promised Grandpa Beebe as they sat at a table in the dining hall at noon. But Grandpa's words sounded bigger than his voice.

The ladies of the auxiliary hovered over them anxiously, heaping their plates with oysters and clam fritters, and great helpings of Chincoteague pot pie.

"Land sakes!" exclaimed a motherly person to Paul and Maureen. "What's the matter with you two young'uns? Such puny appetites! Take my Delbert now, he's on his fourth helping."

But try as they would, Maureen and Paul could not eat. The food that usually tasted so good lodged in their throats. Even Grandpa Beebe had no appetite. "Ef I didn't *know* 'twas plump oysters and rolled-out dumplings with chunks of chicken," he said, "I'd swear I was eatin' bran mash!"

In the afternoon there was the bronco busting. It was like any wild west show, except there were no mountains in the distance. Only fishing boats and the sea, and gulls flying, and a soft wind singing in the pines.

The wild ponies, crazed with fright, were let out of chutes. While the crowds gasped and shrieked, the ponies crow-hopped. They bucked. They threw their riders at once, or

tolerated them for brief seconds. The people cheered madly when an oyster-tonger wearing a red baseball cap and holding a big unlighted cigar in his mouth stayed on his bronco for a matter of minutes. And just when he was doffing his cap and bowing to the crowds, the pony tossed him and his cigar and red cap high into the air.

An instant's pause; then such a whooping and laughter went up as he recovered his cigar and pulled his cap over his face, that it was heard by Grandma in the kitchen at Pony Ranch. Paul and Maureen watched, but they were not really a part of the laughing, cheering crowd.

Thursday night, Friday passed. The Pied Piper and all the brood mares except the Phantom were driven into the channel to swim back to Assateague for another year of freedom.

It was Saturday before Paul and Maureen were able to talk about their loss. They were in the dooryard, taking turns grinding clams for Grandma.

"If only I had never gone on the roundup," Paul said bitterly.

Maureen shook her head. "It was my fault. If only I'd gotten to the grounds at four, 'stead of five!"

"If only I'd told the fire chief the night before."

"What'll we do with the hundred and two dollars?" Maureen asked.

A long silence was broken by the squeaking of the crank.

"We could buy Grandma and Grandpa one of those electric

toasters," Paul said at last. "And we could save the rest to go to college on the mainland when we get grown."

"Let's do it," Maureen agreed, but without much enthusiasm.

Later that morning, as they were looking at electric toasters in a window on Main Street, they heard a man's voice call, "Hi, there!"

They turned around to see a station wagon at the curb, with a man and a small boy in the front seat. The man leaned past the boy and poked his head out of the window.

"Can you tell us where the fire chief lives?" he asked.

"Yes, sir," replied Paul. "He lives up the second street, third house from the corner. But I reckon he's still at the grounds. They're having the drawing on the sorrel this morning."

The boy's head shot out of the car. "The drawing's over," he exclaimed. "And guess what!"

"What?" asked Paul and Maureen.

"I won the pony!" he said breathlessly.

"That's right," nodded the man, who did not seem to share the boy's eagerness. "And now we've got to see the fire chief. He went off in his car before we could find him. By the way," the man questioned, "do you two know him?"

Paul and Maureen managed a smile. "Everybody knows him," they said.

The next moment they spied the chief's car turning in at a gas station on the opposite corner.

"I'll get him for you," Paul said, and he ran across the street.

"Hmm," mused the chief as he limped back with Paul. "Looks to me like Foster, the man from Norfolk. Only before, he didn't have a boy with him."

"Is he the one who bought Misty and Phantom?" Paul asked quickly.

The chief nodded.

By now the man and the boy had gotten out of the station wagon.

"How do," said the fire chief.

"Good morning," replied the man. He took off his hat and began twirling it nervously in his hands. He cleared his throat. Then he pulled a clean white handkerchief from his pocket and wiped his forehead.

"This is Freddy, my young son, and we . . ." He hesitated a moment, then hurried the words, "and we have a problem. You see, the other morning your man Tom sold us a chance on a pony, and I forgot all about it. That is," he laughed, "until this morning when I stopped off at the grounds to show Freddy the tiny foal I had bought for him."

"Tell him, Daddy! Tell him!" interrupted Freddy.

"Just as we stepped out of the car," Mr. Foster continued, "they were raffling off the sorrel colt, and—"

"We won!" shouted Freddy.

"No!" exclaimed the chief, and Paul and Maureen saw the tired look suddenly lift from his face.

"We won! We won!" cried Freddy. "Now tell him the rest, Daddy. Tell him!"

Mr. Foster spoke very quickly now as if the sooner told the better. "You see, sir, Freddy likes the sorrel pony because it is almost the color of my horse. He likes it better than the newborn foal."

Paul and Maureen could hardly breathe. They were staring at Mr. Foster as if they could not believe what they heard.

"Of course," Mr. Foster added, "I appreciate that Pony Penning Day is over and you may not have another chance to sell the little foal. In that case," he said, putting his hat back on his head, "in that case, why—we'll just have to hold to our bargain. Though what we'll do with *two* colts and how we'll get that wild Phantom home has me worried."

There was a long moment of stillness. An old man came along wheeling a cart of squash and watermelons. As the man went by, a dog lying in the doorway of the hardware store thumped his tail noisily. Across the street a juke box was spilling out the words, "Oh, give me a home where the buffalo roam."

Still the chief made no answer. Instead, he hooked his cane over Paul's shoulder. Then he took a notebook out of his

pocket and slowly, carefully, began thumbing through it, reading notations on each page. Finally he tore a leaf out of the book and took a fifty-dollar bill out of his wallet.

Handing the money and the page of writing to Mr. Foster, he said, "There was a boy and a girl had their eyes on the mare and her colt. I can't be sure," he said with a wink, "but I've a mind they still might be interested."

Maureen gave a little gasp. Then she picked up the astonished Freddy and gave him a sound kiss.

"Don't mind her," Paul said to Freddy. "Just girls' fribble." Then he grabbed the fire chief's hand and wrung it until his own ached. He shook hands with Mr. Foster, too, and even with Freddy.

At last he threw back his head like a spirited horse and let out such a loud whinny that it was heard the full length of Chincoteague Island.

Chapter 14

THE WICKIE

USUALLY a colt learns from its mother. It hears her whicker at sound of Man's voice. It sees her gallop to meet him when he comes down to the corral. It sees her lip Man's hand. Soon the colt discovers that Man represents the good things of life—delicious surprises in the way of sugar, carrots, apples. And presently it is trying to please Man, too; not only to be rewarded with something to eat, but to enjoy the tingly feeling of his hand or the pleasant sound of his voice.

With Phantom and Misty things happened the other way around. Misty accepted human beings right from the start.

Their hands felt good to her. She would brace herself, her forelegs splayed out, while Paul or Maureen gently stroked her neck or traced the white blaze on her face. She would lean toward them, asking in the only way she knew that the attentions never stop. Whenever they brushed her foretop or her mane, she lowered her gold eyelashes as if dreaming the most wonderful dreams.

"I declare," chuckled Grandpa. "That Misty 'minds me of a girl gettin' beautified for her first dance!"

Never was a colt more curious! A wickie was something to be investigated. First she nosed it. It tickled her colty whiskers and made her sneeze. Sneezing was fun. And one day, without knowing how it happened, she was wearing the wickie around her neck. It did not hurt! It did not hurt at all. Paul and Maureen were at the other end of it, and they were singing softly,

Come along, little Misty,
Come along.

Misty moved a step toward them, her ears pricked as if to catch the music in her name. And, wonder of wonders, she was rewarded with a lump of sugar as she walked along.

When Phantom saw that Misty was not being hurt, she would come forward, too. Nervously she would take what was offered and then back away, a safe distance behind her colt.

Grandma often came out to watch, with a dish of apples to pare or an armful of clothes to patch.

"This be the topsy-turviest pair I've ever seed!" she would laugh softly. "'Stead of the colt following its mommy, it's t'other way around."

It was days, however, before the Phantom would let anyone touch her. The mere placement of a hand upon her coat acted like an electric shock. She would bolt away, snorting in fright. But as August wore on, the horseflies became so vicious that she turned to Paul and Maureen for help.

"She's missing the surf," Paul said as they watched her trying to shudder her coat to drive the flies away. But the flies seemed to stick faster, drawing blood until Phantom was crazy with pain. They watched her sidle up to the other ponies on the ranch to get the benefit of their swishing tails, but the other ponies bunched up and ran away from her. She tried standing head-to-tail with Misty, but Misty's tail was so short and floppy that it was not much good.

Finally, when she was almost exhausted, she let Paul and Maureen flick the flies for her. She would offer first one leg and then another. And before the fly season was over, she had learned to "shake hands" like any circus pony.

Riding Phantom was quite another matter. Yet it, too, came about so gradually that she was quite unaware how it happened. First Maureen made a wide girth out of an old bedsheet and fitted it around Phantom's body immediately back of her forelegs. Once Phantom discovered that she could gallop just as fast with a band around her body, she no longer minded it. Next, Paul fastened a small sack of sand to the girth. Phantom tried in vain to buck it off, but at last she seemed to realize that she could run as fast as ever with a sack on her back. After that she no longer fought it.

"If she'll carry the sand, she'll carry us!" Paul concluded.

And so it was. By the time frost came, they were riding her bareback, with nothing but a single "come-along" rope made of wickie.

"Phantom just won't take a metal bit in her mouth," Paul explained to Grandpa one evening as he and Maureen stood watching him trim one of his ponies' hooves.

"Great jumping mullets!" Grandpa exploded. "This pinto's forefeet has growed out so far I'm going to need my old-timey razor asides my snips. Maureen, you go git my razor. Now what was it you said about Phantom?" Grandpa asked as he waited.

"She just won't take a metal bit," Paul repeated. "We're still using the old wickie for bit and bridle both."

"Wa-al, ain't she travelin' where you want her to?" Grandpa barked, turning around to look at Paul.

"Oh, yes. We just lean the way we want to go and lay the wickie over against her neck."

"What more do ye want?"

"Nothing, Grandpa. Nothing at all. Maureen and I, we thought you'd be ashamed of us for not doing the job right—on our own pony."

"Ashamed!" bellowed Grandpa, straightening up and rubbing both his ears. "I'm so dang proud it's a wonder I ain't busted my suspender straps. Name me two other kids as has gentled a three-year-old wild mare."

Maureen came running with the razor.

"Walk!" commanded Grandpa. "How often do ye got to be told that if ye want to live to be a grownup ye should never run with anything as sharp as my old-timey razor?"

"Grandpa says it's all right!" Paul told Maureen. "Phantom doesn't ever need to know a metal bit."

"Not ever?" asked Maureen.

"Not ever!" repeated Grandpa as he wielded the razor in an expert manner. "I reckon she'll be happier without ever knowing."

Chapter 15

THE FIRE CHIEF PAYS A CALL

THERE WAS no question about Misty's happiness. She pranced around the ponies that came and went as if she knew that they were temporary guests, while she, Misty, was one of the family. This was her *home*.

When she playfully nipped the older ponies, they would lay back their ears until they saw who it was. Then they would whinny as much as to say, "It was only Misty."

She could be wild as a hare or gentle as a lamb. When the days grew brisk she would *gallumph* across the hard marsh, then suddenly she would stop stock-still, letting a gull light on her back while her nostrils quivered with excitement.

"Do you reckon Phantom is happy, too?" Maureen asked one day when the winter wind blew raw and cold.

"'Course she's happy," replied Paul. "Did you see me ride her down to the point before breakfast? She was neighing for joy. Her hooves hardly touched the earth."

"Oh, I know she's happy then, but . . ."

"But what?"

"Well, sometimes I see her leaning out over the fence—not yearning for the grass on the other side of it, but just looking away toward the White Hills and the sea."

"And is there something . . . ?" Paul asked after a little thought. "Is there something *far away* about her?"

"That's what I mean, Paul."

"I've noticed it, too," Paul admitted. "Sometimes when you can see the wild ponies frisking along Assateague Beach, she seems to be watching them. And it's kind of sad—like the time you wanted the doll with real hair at the carnival and you won the pencil box instead."

Maureen blushed. "Now that I'm grown up, I've almost forgotten about the doll. And Phantom'll forget her young days, too."

"Sure she will. We'll race her every day. She's happy then."

There was no doubt about it. The Phantom was wild with happiness when she raced. She showed it in the arching of her neck, in the upward pluming of her tail, in the flaring of her nostrils. Paul or Maureen had only to close their legs in on her sides to make her surge forward. Then she would skim the earth like the gulls she knew so well.

With the passing days the island folk began to notice her speed.

"Reckon Black Comet's going to have a little competition next Pony Penning," some said, wagging their heads wisely.

Others sneezed at the idea. "Phantom's got too much wildness in her," they said. "She's just as liable to jump the fence as run around the track. You can't depend on them wild ones."

Over in Pocomoke there was talk of the Phantom, too. In the schoolyards, across dinner tables, in the barber shops— everywhere the Phantom's name could be heard.

142

"She's built for speed," one mainlander admitted, "but I still favor Black Comet. He's used to the crowds. He knows how to snug along the fence. He knows how to save his power for the home stretch."

Spring came early to the little sea island. By the first week in April, myrtle bushes were covered over with a yellow fuzz and pine trees wore light-green finger tips to show another year's growth.

Phantom seemed to grow more restless as the season advanced. When Paul and Maureen came home from school they sometimes found her pacing around and around the corral, her head lowered. Other times she stood leaning far out over the fence, and there was a wild, sad look about her.

"Maybe she's looking for us," Maureen would say hopefully.

"Maybe!" nodded Paul.

One late afternoon toward the end of April the fire chief paid a surprise call.

"We 'spected you was coming!" exclaimed Grandma, her round face beaming. "See? Maureen's got a place all laid for ye."

The fire chief smiled. "One—two—three—four—five," he counted the blue-and-white plates around the kitchen table. Then he sniffed the ham baking, and he saw the heaping mound of oysters rolled in eggs and cracker meal and fried a golden brown. He moistened his lips.

"I'm staying!" he said.

There was not much talk while Grandma cut slivers of pink ham, dished up the oysters, and ladled hot gravy over the dumplings. And there was even less while everyone ate his fill.

At last the fire chief pushed his plate aside and lighted his pipe. "I've really come to see the owners of the Phantom," he said between puffs. "Wonder if they'd be interested in . . ."

At exactly that moment the fire chief's pipe went out and he had to stop in the middle of what he had to say. Slowly he found a match and relit it.

Paul's and Maureen's eyes were fixed on the chief's. They leaned forward on the very edge of their chairs.

"Wonder if they'd be interested in . . ." he stopped to puff and puff.

"Yes?" questioned Paul quickly.

"In racing the Phantom against Black Comet."

Paul's eyes caught Maureen's. Then their faces broke into a grin.

"Ho-ho-ho," chortled Grandpa. "I don't know who the joke's on. But these two been expectin' to race Phantom ever since last Pony Pennin'."

"Even before that," Maureen said gleefully. "Why, that morning over on Assateague when we first saw the Phantom, we talked about it even then."

Paul blushed. "Guess we just took it for granted you'd ask us."

The fire chief laughed heartily. "Well, now it's settled for sure," he said as he stood up to go. "Lucy Lee can't run this year. She'll be having a new colt along about then. And Patches has been sold to a dealer. So it'll be the Phantom against Black Comet and Delbert's chestnut filly, Firefly."

"And may the best hoss win!" prayed Grandpa as he nervously fingered the bristles of his ear.

Chapter 16

THE PULLY BONE

THE NEXT three months were filled with excitement for Phantom and her owners. Paul and Maureen were conditioning her for the big race. They fed her more liberally on grain. They rode her three miles each day, starting off at a slow jog, then trotting her, then asking for a burst of speed midway of the ride, then slowly jogging her back home again.

It was the early morning when the world was all red and gold with the rising sun that Paul and Maureen chose for Phantom's training period. They would take turns riding her —across the tundra-like beach, hard packed after a rain; up

147

and down Main Street, where her hooves sounded like sea shells pinging against the pavement; over trails carpeted with pine needles, where she made no sound at all.

They rode her out to the pony penning grounds, getting her used to the feel of the track and the sight of the white fence.

Before long the Phantom came to be a familiar and glorious sight. Her fame grew and spread. Now, on pleasant Sundays, visitors from the mainland began coming to see her.

Misty grew jealous of the attentions her mother was getting. She would nose in, trying to nip the buttons from the men's coats or the flowers on the ladies' hats. One time she

lifted a hat all covered over with roses and dropped it in the water barrel.

This brought Grandpa Beebe running with a handful of gunnysacks. He pretended to be angry as he rescued the dripping hat and tried to dry it off with the sacks. "Paul and Maureen!" he would shout in his thunderous voice. "Hain't you never going to drive any sense into that Misty's head? She'll grow up thinkin' she's a baby all her days. Never seed a critter so mettlesome!"

As July came in and Pony Penning Day drew near, something came between Paul and Maureen. If Paul worked around the barnyard, Maureen made some excuse to go off down to the oyster boats to see if the men had brought up any sea stars in their oyster tongs. And if Maureen worked at home for Grandpa or Grandma, Paul went off treading clams for Kim Horsepepper or catching sea horses.

"What's the matter 'twixt Paul and Maureen?" Grandma asked Grandpa one night after the house was still.

"I don't know fer sure, mind ye, but I suspicion it's about the race," Grandpa replied.

"Why, I thought 'twas all settled. Hain't the Phantom goin' to run?"

"A-course. But the catch is—who's to ride her?"

"They both hankering to ride?" questioned Grandma.

"That's my guess," Grandpa nodded.

Finally, on the Monday morning before Pony Penning, Grandma asked the question right out. She and Maureen were hanging up clothes at the time, while Paul, perched on top of a chicken coop, was silently whittling a pole into a clothes prop.

"Which of ye," Grandma said, as she removed a clothespin from her mouth, "which of ye will ride Phantom in the big race?"

A long silence was the only answer.

"Well! Well!" said Grandma brightly. "If ye won't state yer rathers, I got a fine idea."

Still no answer. Maureen shook the creases out of a table-

cloth as if her life depended on it. Paul kept on whittling furiously.

Just then Grandpa Beebe came by. He glanced around sharply. "Why's everyone so hushed?" he asked. "Except fer the flappin' of the clothes I'd think 'twas Sunday meetin'-time."

"Why, I just asked who's to ride Phantom come Pony Penning Day," replied Grandma, hanging her clothespin bag on the line and looking from one to the other.

"Oh," and Grandpa strung the little word out until it seemed to have springs in it. He dropped the posthole digger he was carrying and toed it with his boots.

Seconds went by.

"If I wasn't in my seventy-three," he shook his finger, "if I wasn't in my seventy-three going on my seventy-four, I'd settle the hull matter and ride her myself."

Grandma straightened up from the clothesbasket.

"Clarence!" she said, speaking loud enough so her voice would reach Paul. "Seems like somethin' told me to save the pully bone from that marsh hen. It's hangin' above the almanac in the kitchen."

Grandpa slapped his thigh. "Nothin' could be fairer than a pully bone!" he exclaimed. "The one that breaks off the biggest part gits to ride."

"I'll fetch it," Maureen called over her shoulder as she disappeared into the kitchen. She came out holding one end of the wishbone very gingerly, as though it might break off in her hand.

"Now then!" Grandpa cleared his throat nervously.

Grandma picked up the empty clothesbasket, then set it down again in the very same spot.

"Now then," Grandpa repeated, "stop that gol-durn whittlin' and step up, Paul."

Paul's legs seemed as wobbly as a colt's. He came forward very slowly, and his hand shook as he grasped the other end of the wishbone with his thumb and forefinger.

"Squinch yer eyes tight," Grandma directed. "Make yer wish. And when I count three, *pull!*"

Paul and Maureen each took a long, deep breath as they clutched the tiny wishbone that was to decide their fate.

"One," Grandma counted slowly. "Two it is—and three!"

With a slight cracking noise, the wishbone broke. The larger half was in Paul's hand.

He gave a whistle of joy. Then his face sobered as he caught sight of Maureen, who was burying her half of the wishbone in the sandy soil. She looked up, trying to cover her feelings with a little smile.

"You won, Paul," she said, blinking. "You'll ride her better anyhow."

Chapter 17

WINGS ON HER FEET

THE LAST Wednesday in July dawned hot and still. Another Pony Penning Day had come!

By sunup the causeway between the mainland and Chincoteague was choked with traffic—trucks, station wagons, jeeps, cars of every description, bringing visitors to the island. They watched excitedly as the wild ponies swam ashore after the roundup. They lined the streets to see the procession to the pens; they cheered the bronco busters. But even after these events were over, the crowds kept on coming. For this year the big event was the race. Phantom was running! A wild sea horse against the sleek, well-trained Black Comet, winner for three years.

Toward evening a light wind came up, whisking sheep clouds before it. The sun was a huge red balloon hovering over the bay as Paul and Maureen, riding double on Phantom, turned into the pony penning grounds.

Maureen slid to her feet, and before she could whisper a word of encouragement into the Phantom's ear she was caught like a fly in a web. Her schoolmates, her uncles and aunts— everyone wanted to be with her during the race. They felt sorry for her because she was not riding. They seemed to wrap themselves about her until she could hardly breathe. Oh, how she longed to be by herself! Then she could race *with* Paul and the Phantom! Only by being alone could she *be* Paul and Phantom both.

It was the voice over the loud speaker that came to her rescue. "Tonight, ladies and gentlemen!" the voice blared. "Tonight Black Comet from Pocomoke races against Firefly and the Phantom."

Everyone began running toward the track. Maureen slipped away from her friends and lost herself in the crowds. She wedged her way into a small opening between strangers and soon she was standing at the rails, her stomach against a fence post. She heard strange voices all about her. But now there was no need to listen to them. They were as unimportant as the little insect voices of the night.

She drew a deep breath as the names of the three entries were announced again.

"There comes Black Comet!" the cry went up on all sides. "There he is!"

She saw Black Comet amble out on the track, aloof and black as night. He seemed bored with the entire business. Maureen would not have been surprised to see him yawn.

Now Firefly, a tall, rangy mare, pranced nervously to the starting post. Maureen's eyes passed over her lightly, then lingered on the Phantom who was parading to the post with dignity in her manner. She seemed unaware of the crowds, as

if for her they did not exist. Her head was uplifted, her nose testing the winds, her body trembling. She could not understand the delay. She snuffed the wind hungrily. The wind was calling her, yet Paul was holding her back.

At last the signal was given. A roar went up from the crowd. "They're off!"

"Black Comet at the rail," came the clipped voice over the loud speaker, "Phantom on the outside. But it's Firefly who's taking the lead!"

From then on no one could hear the announcer for all the yelling. The changeable crowds were calling, "Firefly! Firefly!"

Firefly held the lead the first quarter, then Black Comet shot forward and pulled out in front.

Maureen dug her fingernails into the fence rail. "Phantom!" she prayed. ' Oh, Phantom! Get a-going! It's a race."

But the Phantom was not running a race. She was enjoying herself. She was a piece of thistledown borne by the wind, moving through space in wild abandon. She was coming up, not to pass Firefly and Black Comet, but for the joy of flying. Her legs went like music. She was sweeping past Firefly now. She was less than a length behind Black Comet.

The people climbed up on the fence rails in a frenzy of excitement.

"Come on, Black Comet!" screamed the crowds from Pocomoke. "Come on!"

"Gee-up, Phantom!" cried the island folk.

Maureen was no longer an onlooker. She was the Phantom winging around the curve, her nostrils fire-red in the dying sun. She was Paul, leaning forward in a kind of wild glory.

She was drawing close to Black Comet. Now she was even. She was sailing ahead. She was over the finish line. She was winner by a length!

The crowds grew hysterical. "It's Phantom! Phantom! She won!" But there was no stopping the Phantom! She was flying on around the track.

The voice over the loud speaker was laughing. "Only once around," it was saying. "Only once around." Paul pulled back on the wickie and spoke softly in Phantom's ear. Gradually he brought her to a stop.

Maureen was laughing and crying too. The crowds pushed past her, dived between the rails, flocked around the Phantom. They yelled and thumped one another on the back as the judge handed Paul a purse.

Paul felt of its bulging contents. Then his eyes swept the crowds.

"Here—here I am!" cried Maureen.

Every eye turned to see whom Paul wanted. When they discovered Maureen, standing on the top rail of the fence like a bird on a twig, friends and strangers, too, clapped and cheered. In an instant Paul was riding through the little opening they had made. With the fence as a mounting block, Maureen swung up behind Paul.

The island folk went mad with happiness.

"Hoo-ray for Paul and Maureen!"

"Hoo-ray for the Phantom!" they rejoiced.

But Paul and Maureen found only one face in all that sea of faces and heard only one voice in all that blur of noise. It was Grandpa Beebe's. "Git home," he bellowed. "Tell Grandma."

All the way home Paul talked to the Phantom. "Do you know," he murmured, "do you know you won twelve whole dollars? And we're going to spend it all on you?"

"We could buy her red plumes, and ribbons to braid in her mane," suggested Maureen.

Paul leaned far forward to get as close as he could to Phantom's ear. "We could buy you shiny brass and leather trappings," he said. "You could be handsomer than any horse in the king's guard."

The Phantom let out a long whinny into the deepening twilight.

Paul laughed and laughed. "Want to know what she said?"

"What'd she say, Paul?"

"She said, 'Buy that toaster for Grandma and Grandpa. As for me,' she said, 'all I want is wings on my feet!'"

Chapter 18

A WILD BUGLE

I T RAINED fitfully during the night following the race. By morning the rain stopped and the sun broke through softly in slanting rays, drawing the moisture upward in thick curtains of mist.

After the excitement of the day before, matters on Pony Ranch were settling down to their usual routine. Paul and Maureen were busy with chores, Paul repairing the chicken house and Maureen scrubbing the water pans. Misty tagged first one, then the other—like a puppy with two masters.

Close to the fence stood the Phantom. She kept lifting her head upward, as if to worship the miracle of the sun drawing water. From time to time Paul took sidelong glances at her.

"Let's take turns racing her as soon as our chores are done," he called to Maureen. "You can be first."

Maureen smiled to herself. She knew that Paul was trying to make it up to her for not riding in the race. She hurried with her chores. Then, with Misty at her heels, she hung her apron on the clothesline and went to get the wickie.

When the Phantom caught sight of the wickie she whinnied, then stood trembling while Maureen slipped the rope-like root between her teeth, brought it under her chin and tied a square knot. It was strange how gentle Phantom could be. But even in her gentleness there was a wilding look in her eye, as if only her body were inside the corral while her real self lived somewhere far away.

Grabbing Phantom's mane, Maureen jumped onto her back.

"Ready!" she called to Paul.

Paul dropped his hammer and came running to let down the bars of the gate which fitted into horseshoes nailed to the fence posts. Phantom pawed the ground nervously as if irked by Paul's slowness.

With one bar down, Maureen put her heels into Phantom's side and Phantom sailed over the hurdle and out upon the marshy plain.

164

Misty tried to follow but Paul pushed her back. "Soon we'll be racing you, too," he promised, combing her foretop with his fingers. "But today we got to make Phantom happy."

Then he carefully replaced the top bars, climbed over the fence and wandered out to a lone pine tree. There he stood, leaning up against the tree, waiting his turn. His blood quickened as he watched Phantom whip across the little point of land that went down to meet the sea. Around and across and up and down the flat tongue of land she swept, like the sea mews that soared overhead.

At last Paul waved them in. "My turn now!"

At exactly the moment when Maureen turned Phantom over to Paul there was the sound of a ringing neigh in the distance. It speared the morning stillness. It seemed to come, not from the sea, but from the Spanish galleon, back across the ages.

Phantom's ears pricked. She jerked her head in the direction of Assateague Island. Tremblingly she listened. The bugle came again, strong and clear. It brought Grandpa Beebe bounding over the gate, running toward Phantom.

"It's the Pied Piper!" he yelled. "He's coming to git the Phantom."

Paul and Maureen strained their eyes toward the island of Assateague, but all they could see were the white spumes from the billows, and skeins of mist rising from the sea. Then suddenly one of the whitecaps seemed to be flying free. It was the foaming mane of the Pied Piper, racing in with the billows.

"Git on Phantom's back!" Grandpa called. "Whup her, Paul! Whup her hard! Maureen! Git that gate open!"

Her heart pounding, Maureen flew to the gate. As fast as she could, she let the bars down, at the same time shoving Misty back. "Paul!" she cried. "Get a handful of her mane. Ride her toward Misty."

With a gasp of anguish she looked back. Paul was not trying to hold Phantom. He was slipping the wickie out of her mouth. He was giving Phantom her freedom.

"Oh, Paul!" screamed Maureen. "Hold her! Hold her! Don't let her go!" But her words were lost. The Phantom's whinnies were high with excitement. The Pied Piper was heading straight for her, his neck thrust forward, his head down, his eyes hidden by that long creamy foretop.

Grandpa waved his hat, trying to head him off, his arms whirling like a windmill. The Pied Piper veered around him. Then he snorted and trumpeted to the heavens.

"Paul!" bellowed Grandpa. "You'll be tromped down. Git outen the way!"

But Paul stood there as if caught in the Pied Piper's spell.

For a moment the Phantom hesitated. She looked obediently to Paul, her master. Then that wild bugle sounded again. It seemed to awaken some force within her, creating a curious urging in her mind. A shudder of excitement went through her. She twisted her body high in the air as if she were shaking herself free—free of fences that imprisoned, free of lead ropes, free of stalls that shut out the smell of pines and the sound of the sea.

An impatient whinny escaped her. She whirled past Paul, then ran flying to meet the Pied Piper.

The air went wild with greeting. Deep rumbling neighs. High joyous whickers. The stallion and the mare were brushing each other with their noses, talking together in soft little grunts

and snorts as animals will. At last the Pied Piper nipped her thigh, urging her forward. This time the Phantom did not hesitate. She flew toward her island home. Only once she turned her head as if she were looking backward.

"Take good care of my baby," she seemed to say. "She belongs to the world of men, but I—I belong to the isle of the wild things!"

For long seconds, Paul and Grandpa and Maureen stood stock-still. They watched the Pied Piper plunge into the surf until he seemed part of the flying foam. They watched the Phantom until all they could see was the white map on her withers. Then the map smalled until it, too, was lost among the whitecaps of the sea.

The air about them quivered like a violin string. Then suddenly the string snapped, and the everyday world was all about once more. Grandpa was no longer the wiry man who had bounded over the fence. He was himself, gnarled and a little stiff-legged as he walked to the gate. Paul followed along behind him, and some of the Phantom's happiness seemed to shine in his face. He had given her the freedom she longed for.

Maureen lowered the bars of the gate for them, then put them back in place.

With one accord the old man and the boy and girl went to the Phantom's stall. It was not empty. Misty's quizzical little face with its funny blaze was peering around at them. She came trotting out of the door and gave Paul's face a great

swipe with her wet tongue. It was as if she had said, "Why is everyone so quiet? I'm here. Me! Misty!"

She reached out for Maureen, too, and as Maureen turned her cheek to be nuzzled, she noticed a few copper-colored hairs from Phantom's tail caught in the half-door of the stall. Winding them into a circlet, she fastened them above the manger.

"Guess she was just a Phantom after all," Maureen spoke quietly.

"'Course she was," Paul said.

Grandpa began working hard at the bristles in his ears. "Ye done the right thing, children," he said huskily. "Phantom wuz never what you'd call happy. She belongs to Assateague. But Misty here, she belongs to us."

At mention of her name, Misty sidled over to Grandpa and scratched her head up and down against his broad shoulder

How good it was to be the center of attention! She went from one to the other, butting her face gently against Paul's pocket, asking for a kernel of corn, lipping Maureen, nipping the brim of Grandpa's battered old hat.

"Phantom was a good mammy," Maureen said. "She stayed with her baby as long as she needed to. Colts got to grow up sometime," she declared, her thoughts slipping back to what the fire chief had said.

Misty seemed to sense the importance of this moment. She backed away from the group, her head uplifted, not toward the sea and the island of Assateague, but inland, toward the well-pounded trails of Chincoteague. Her whole body quivered as if she saw a promise of great things to come—of races won, of foals tagging at her side. Overcome by all the excitement in store, she kicked her heels in ecstasy and let out a high, full whinny of joy. It sounded for all the world like explosive laughter.

Paul gave a little gasp.

"What did she say?" Maureen asked quickly.

"I never!" Paul's eyes widened in disbelief.

Grandpa clapped his hat far down on his head. "Land sakes, Paul! You never what?"

"Reckon I never heard a pony talk up so plain. Why, she just laughed deep down inside her. 'I'm Misty of Chincoteague,' she said, plainer'n any words."

173

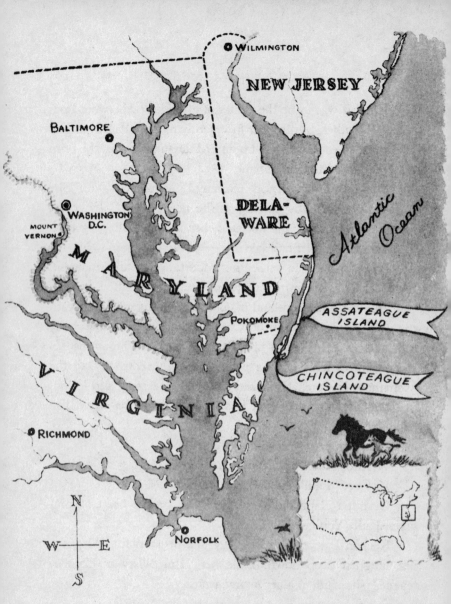

Four miles off the eastern shore of Virginia lies the tiny, wind-rippled isle of Chincoteague. It is only seven miles long and averages but twenty-one inches above the sea.

Assateague Island, however, is thirty-three miles long. Just as Paul Beebe says, Assateague is an outrider, protecting little Chincoteague from the rough seas of the Atlantic. The outer island is a wildlife refuge for wild geese and ducks and the wild ponies.

For their help the author is grateful to

VICTORIA PRUITT, Island Historian, Chincoteague Island

MRS. W. E. DAVIS, known to everyone as Miss Mollie, Chincoteague Island

CAPTAIN JACK RICHARDSON, for many years with the United States Coast Guard on Assateague Island

BOB WILLIAMS, who helped me find people and places, Chincoteague Island

ALFRED TAPSELL, seventeen years before the mast in the British Merchant Service

WAYNE DINSMORE, Secretary, Horse Association of America

J. NORMAN JOHNSON, Meteorologist, U. S. Weather Bureau

MILTON C. RUSSELL, Head, Reference and Circulation Section, Virginia State Library

H. H. HEWITT and ROBERTA SUTTON, Chicago Public Library

DR. CHESTER J. ATTIG, late Head of the History Department, North Central College

C. E. GODSHALK, Director, the Morton Arboretum

MARY ALICE JONES, Children's Book Editor, Rand McNally & Company

MR. AND MRS. ROBERT H. QUAYLE, Wayne, Illinois

LOUISE COFFIN, Wayne, Illinois

GRACE LUENZMANN, Wayne, Illinois

ROBERT V. NEVINS, Brookville, Massachusetts

JUNE BECKMAN, Naperville, Illinois

GERTRUDE JUPP, Milwaukee, Wisconsin

MR. AND MRS. L. C. FERGUSON, Hammond, New York